WINDOWS® 98
FOR BEGINNERS

Anna Milbourne

Illustrated by Christyan Fox
Designed by Isaac Quaye and Zöe Wray

Additional design by Andrea Slane • Cover by Isaac Quaye
Edited by Gillian Doherty

Technical consultant: David Taylor • Managing editor: Philippa Wingate
Managing designer: Stephen Wright • Illustrations using Microsoft® Paint: Maria Pearson
Editorial assistance: Fiona Patchett • Design assistance: Nicola Butler

Contents

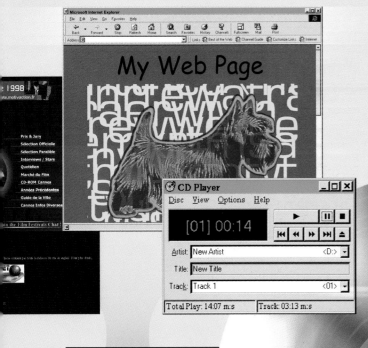

Introducing Windows® 98

This book introduces Microsoft® Windows® 98, and explains in easy steps how you can use it both practically and creatively. If you don't have Windows® 98 on your computer already, turn to page 76 for information about how to put it onto your computer.

What is Windows® 98?

Windows® 98 is a type of computer operating system. An operating system controls the way your computer works and allows you to give your computer instructions about what you want it to do. Windows® 98 is easy to use because it shows information as pictures and words on your computer screen.

Using this book

If you have not used a computer or the operating system called Windows® 95 before, start at the beginning of the book and go through it in order. The book shows you how to do things step by step, with the later pages building on skills you have learned along the way.

If you have used Windows® 95 before, you can flick through the book to find sections that interest you. There is a symbol (see the key below) to help you find out about the features that are new to Windows® 98.

Problem solving

There is a glossary on page 78 where you can look up words you don't understand. If you get stuck, Windows® 98 has its own help system. Find out how to use it on page 74.

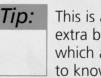

Key

Look out for the following symbols throughout the book:

⚠️ This is a Warning box. It contains important information which can help prevent problems.

Tip: This is a Tip box. It contains extra bits of information which are useful or fun to know.

98 This symbol marks sections that contain information about new or updated features in Windows® 98.

Welcome to your desktop

This section introduces the first things that you will see on your screen in Windows® 98 when you switch on your computer. It tells you about the items that appear, and what they are for.

To begin

When you switch on your computer, Windows® 98 starts automatically. As your computer is starting up, you will see lots of lines of text flashing onto your screen. After this, a coloured screen with the Microsoft® Windows® 98 logo on it will appear. This is called the opening screen.

The desktop

When the opening screen disappears, it is replaced by another coloured display. This is your desktop. You will see a tiny picture of an egg-timer somewhere on your screen, which means that your computer is busy getting ready for you to use. When the egg-timer symbol disappears, your computer is ready.

Your computer desktop, like a real desktop, is a workspace containing tools you can use to help you work. The little pictures on the desktop are called icons. They represent some of the information stored on your computer.

The picture on page 5 shows a typical desktop, and explains what the icons are for. Don't worry if your desktop doesn't look exactly the same as this one – you can change the way it looks (see page 40).

My Computer
You can use this to look at the information that is stored on your computer (see page 28).

My Documents 98
You can keep all of your own work here (see page 18).

Connect to the Internet 98
This helps you gain access to information stored on computers around the world (see page 53).

Network Neighborhood
You can use this to access information on other computers that are connected to yours.

Recycle Bin
You can use this to delete work you don't need any more (see page 35).

MSN
This enables you to connect to Microsoft's information service.

My Briefcase
This can be used to carry information between computers that are not connected to each other.

Online Services 98
This offers details of companies which can connect your computer to others around the world (see page 52).

Start button
You can access almost everything you need to use in Windows® 98 using this button (see page 8).

Quick Launch bar 98
This offers a quick way of accessing certain tools and information on your computer.

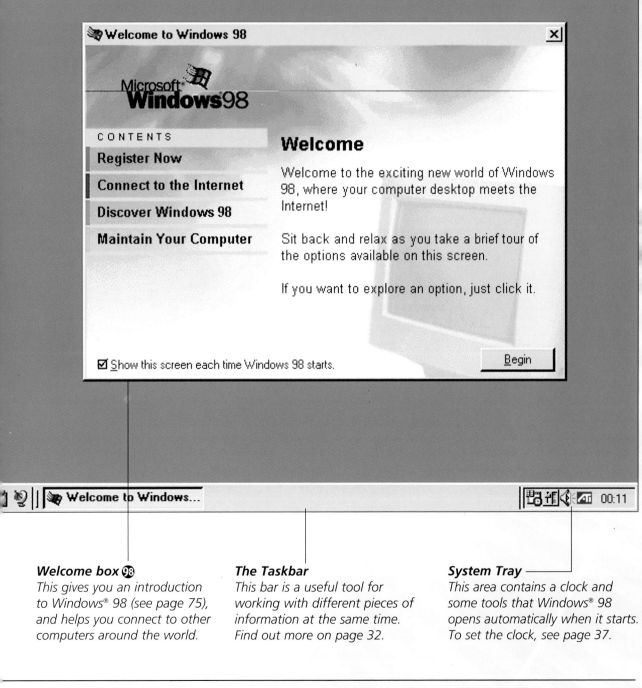

Welcome box 98
This gives you an introduction to Windows® 98 (see page 75), and helps you connect to other computers around the world.

The Taskbar
This bar is a useful tool for working with different pieces of information at the same time. Find out more on page 32.

System Tray
This area contains a clock and some tools that Windows® 98 opens automatically when it starts. To set the clock, see page 37.

Mastering your mouse

The most important tool for using Windows® 98 is your mouse. Windows® 98 works by presenting information to you as pictures and words on your computer screen. This is the display. By moving your mouse, you can use the display to tell your computer what to do.

Mouse buttons

There are different types of mice. All mice have at least two buttons. Some also have a wheel or a third button. These make certain tasks easier to do, but you can do everything you need using the outer two buttons of your mouse. If your mouse has a wheel, find out how to use it on page 10.

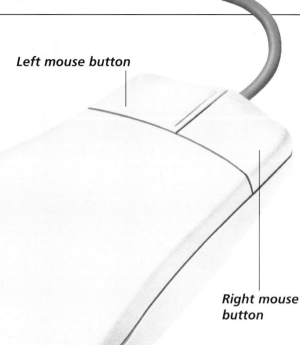

Left mouse button

Right mouse button

This is a computer mouse. It gets its name from its shape and tail-like cable.

A mouse with a wheel is called a scrolling mouse.

Wheel

A few pointers

You will see a little arrow on your display which looks like the first of the symbols shown below. This is the pointer. By moving your mouse across a flat surface, you can make the pointer move on your display. The pointer symbol changes according to which part of the display it is resting over, or what kind of task the computer is carrying out.

Here are some of the different pointer symbols.

Alternative tools

Any tool which you use to work with a computer's display is called a pointing device. A mouse is the most common type of pointing device. Portable computers tend to have other types of pointing device, which work differently from a mouse. Two examples are shown below: a touchpad and a trackball. You use a touchpad by running your finger over the pad. To use a trackball, you roll the ball and press the buttons.

Here are two examples of pointing devices.

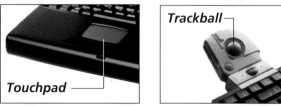

Trackball

Touchpad

Mouse moves

There are different ways in which you can use your mouse to tell your computer what you want it to do. Below are the main techniques you will need to know.

Point   To point at an icon, move the pointer on your display until it is resting over the icon. Try pointing at different icons on the display. If you let the pointer rest over an 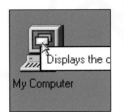 icon for a few seconds, an information box, or ToolTip, will appear. This ToolTip tells you what the icon is for.

Click   To click on something, point at it, then press and release the left mouse button once. Try clicking on the My Computer icon. It will change colour, which  means it is selected. Selecting an icon tells the computer that you want to use that icon. To deselect an icon, click on a blank area of the desktop.

Right-click   To right-click on something, click on it once using the right mouse button. Try right-clicking on the My Computer icon. A list called a context menu will appear near the icon. It offers choices about the particular item you right-clicked on. To close the context menu, click on a blank area of the desktop.

Tip: Different moves ⑱

Windows® 98 allows you to change the way you use your mouse to work with your display.

There are two different ways of doing this: Classic Style or Web Style. The automatic setting on your computer is called Classic Style. The mouse moves described here are also for Classic Style. If you use Web Style, the mouse actions work differently. Find out more about Web Style on page 66.

Double-click   To double-click on something, click on it quickly twice, using the left mouse button. Double-clicking is a short-  hand way of doing certain tasks. Try double-clicking on the My Computer icon. A box will open. (To close the box, click on the cross in its top, right-hand corner.) If it doesn't work, you may not be double-clicking fast enough. You can find out on page 44 how to change the speed at which you need to double-click.

Drag and drop   You can move items on your display. This is called dragging and dropping. To drag an icon, point at it, and press the  left mouse button. Keeping the button pressed down, move the mouse. The icon will move on the display. Release the mouse button to drop the icon in the new position. Some computers may be set so that the icon jumps back into line with the others.

Starting up and shutting down

To do any activity on your computer, such as writing a letter or playing a game, you have to use a program. Each program gives your computer instructions for carrying out a certain set of tasks. You can open most of the programs you will need using the Start menu.

The Start menu

To open the Start menu, click on the *Start* button on your desktop. The Start menu is a list of options, each of which enables you to carry out a different sort of task, such as opening programs, or shutting your computer down when you have finished using it. The picture below shows you what each option on the menu is for. To close the menu, click on the *Start* button again.

This is the Start menu. The labels tell you where to find out more about each item on the menu.

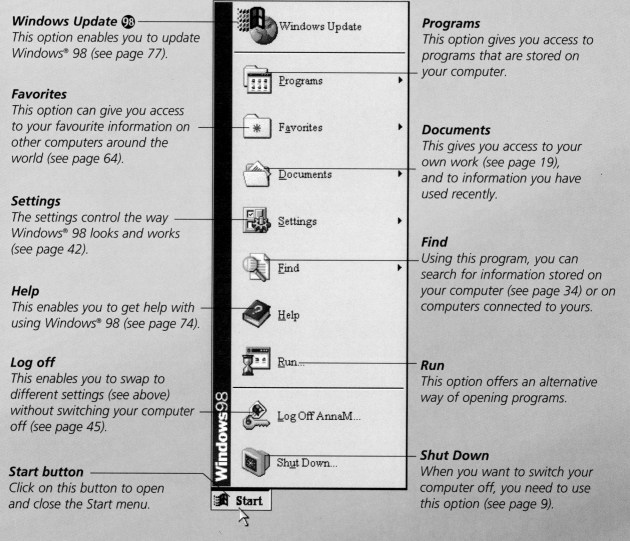

Windows Update
This option enables you to update Windows® 98 (see page 77).

Favorites
This option can give you access to your favourite information on other computers around the world (see page 64).

Settings
The settings control the way Windows® 98 looks and works (see page 42).

Help
This enables you to get help with using Windows® 98 (see page 74).

Log off
This enables you to swap to different settings (see above) without switching your computer off (see page 45).

Start button
Click on this button to open and close the Start menu.

Programs
This option gives you access to programs that are stored on your computer.

Documents
This gives you access to your own work (see page 19), and to information you have used recently.

Find
Using this program, you can search for information stored on your computer (see page 34) or on computers connected to yours.

Run
This option offers an alternative way of opening programs.

Shut Down
When you want to switch your computer off, you need to use this option (see page 9).

More menus

Some of the options on the Start menu have an arrowhead beside them. If you point at one of these options by resting your pointer over it, another menu, known as a submenu, will open. Arrowheads in submenus lead to further submenus.

Arrowheads on menus lead to submenus.

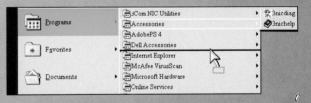

Submenu

Arrowhead

Submenu

Explore the Start menu

Try exploring the Start menu by pointing at different options. You can open any option without an arrowhead by clicking on its name. Try opening a program called Paint, (see page 20). To do this, point at Programs on the Start menu until a submenu opens. Then point at Accessories. Another submenu will open with Paint listed on it. Click on *Paint* to open the program. A box will appear on your display. To close the program, click on the cross, or Close button, in the top, right-hand corner of the box.

Close button

Dragging items on a menu ➒➑

You can change the order in which options appear on the *Programs* submenus by dragging them. Try dragging one of the icons up or down the list. As you drag it, you will see a black line, which shows you the new position of the item on the list. When the black line shows the position you want, drop the item by releasing the mouse button. The item will jump to its new position.

This shows the Accessories icon being dragged downwards on the Programs submenu.

Shut down

You should never switch off your computer without instructing it to shut down first. Shutting down enables your computer to store everything properly before it is switched off. To shut your computer down, open the Start menu and click on *Shut Down*. The box shown below will appear. Click on the words *Shut down*, then click on *OK*. Your computer may switch itself off. If not, a message will appear telling you that you can switch off your computer.

Always use this box to shut down your computer before switching it off.

Working with windows

When you open a program, a box will appear on your display. This is a window. A window is a workspace in which you use a program. The basic features of a window are always the same. This section introduces them, and shows you how to work with windows.

Open a window

To open a window, you need to open a program. Try opening My Computer, by double-clicking on its icon on your desktop. A window similar to the one below will appear on your desktop. A button will also appear on your Taskbar (see page 5) to show that you have a program open.

This shows what different parts of a window are called.

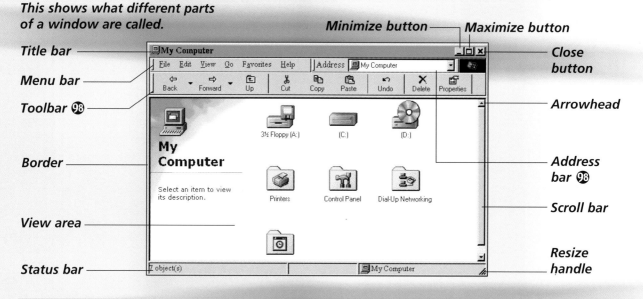

Window bars

Some of the bars on a window enable you to work with the window. Others display information about the window.

Title bar   This shows the name of the open program.
Menu bar   This contains lists of options, or menus, which you can use to work with the open program (see page 12).
Toolbar   This gives easy access to some options from menus in the Menu bar.
Scroll bars   If a window is too small to show all of its contents at once, it will

have scroll bars along the side or the bottom of the window. To look at a different area of the window's contents, drag a scroll bar. This is called scrolling. To scroll a tiny distance at a time, click on one of the arrowheads on the scroll bar. If you have a scrolling mouse you can scroll by turning the wheel.
Status bar   This gives information about the open program.
Address bar   You can use this to change the window's contents without closing the window (see page 29).

Resize and move your windows

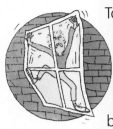

To make windows easier to work with, you can change their size, shape and position on your desktop. For example, you can make a window bigger, so that you have more space to work in it, or smaller, to move it out of the way.

Make a window bigger You can make a window fill your display. This is called maximizing. To do this, click on the Maximize button. The Maximize button will be replaced by another button, called the Restore button. Click on this button to change the window back to its original size and position on your display.

A maximized window has a Restore button instead of a Maximize button.

Shrink a window If a window is getting in the way, you can shrink it so that it appears on your display only as a button on your Taskbar. This is called minimizing. To minimize a window, click on its Minimize button. A minimized window is shown below. To restore the window to its original size and shape, click on this button. A minimized window is still open; it just takes up less room on your display.

A minimized window appears on the Taskbar as a button which looks like this.

My Computer

Change a window's shape As long as a window has not been maximized or minimized, you can change its shape by dragging its borders.

To do this, position your pointer over a border. The pointer will change into a double-headed arrow, as shown below. Drag the border to change the window's shape. You can change a window's width and length at the same time by dragging its Resize handle.

Change the width and length of a window at once by dragging its Resize handle.

Move a window If a window has not been maximized or minimized, you can move it around on your display. Use its Title bar to drag it. To do this, click on the Title bar, hold the left mouse button down, and drag the window to a new position.

Close a window

To close a program that you have finished with, you must close its window. To close a window, click on the Close button in its top, right-hand corner.

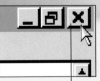

This is the Close button.

Tip: Which is which? 98

If you point at any of the buttons on the right-hand side of the Title bar, a ToolTip will appear to remind you what the button is for.

11

Making choices

When using Windows® 98, you can give your computer instructions by choosing from the various options offered to you. These options are presented in different ways, depending on what kind of choice is available. This section introduces the main sorts of options you will come across, and explains how to make choices.

Menu options

Some choices are presented as menus. A menu is a list of options, which you can open by clicking on its name on the Menu bar of a window. Close a menu by clicking on its name again, or clicking outside the menu on your display. To choose an option from a menu, click on it. This is called selecting. The picture below shows an open menu. The labels describe different ways of using the menu to make choices.

This is an open menu. The labels describe how to use it to make choices.

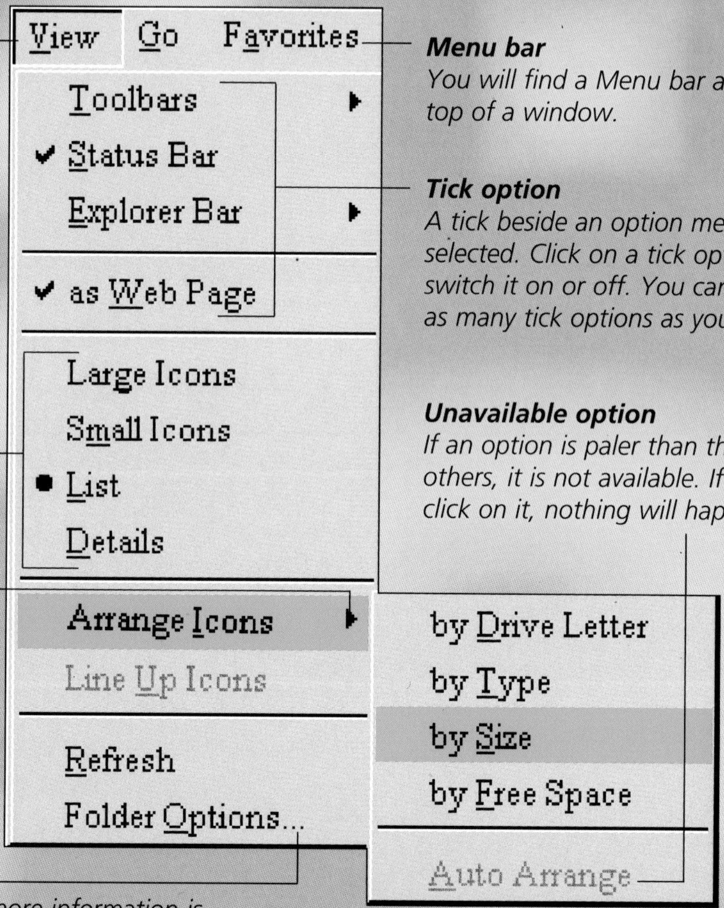

Menu name
To open or close a menu, click on its name on the Menu bar of an open window.

Button option
A large dot, or button, beside an option means it is selected. You can only select one button option at a time in one section of a menu. Click on an option to select it. The option selected previously will switch itself off.

Arrowhead
An arrowhead means that another menu, or submenu, will open from this option. Point at the option to open the submenu.

Three dots
Three dots beside an option mean more information is needed. If you click on this option, a box, called a dialog box, will appear (see page 13).

Menu bar
You will find a Menu bar at the top of a window.

Tick option
A tick beside an option means it is selected. Click on a tick option to switch it on or off. You can choose as many tick options as you like.

Unavailable option
If an option is paler than the others, it is not available. If you click on it, nothing will happen.

View   Go   Favorites

Toolbars ▶
✓ Status Bar
Explorer Bar ▶

✓ as Web Page

Large Icons
Small Icons
● List
Details

Arrange Icons ▶
Line Up Icons

Refresh
Folder Options...

by Drive Letter
by Type
by Size
by Free Space

Auto Arrange

Dialog boxes

If Windows® 98 needs more information before carrying out a set of instructions, a box will appear on your display. This is a dialog box. A dialog box often has different sections that you need to fill in, like a questionnaire. You can make choices by clicking on options. Sometimes you will need to type some information in.

Radio buttons   If you can only choose one option at once, the choice is usually displayed as options with circles by them. These are radio buttons. Radio buttons work in a similar way to button options on a menu. An option with a black dot beside it is selected. To select a different option, click on it. The option selected previously will switch off automatically.

This is an example of some radio buttons.

Drop-down lists   An arrowhead next to a box means it contains a list of options. Click on the arrowhead to open the list. To choose an option from the list, click on it. A drop-down list is shown below.

Instead of opening a list to choose an option, you can sometimes type information into the box. To do this, click on the box and then type in the information.

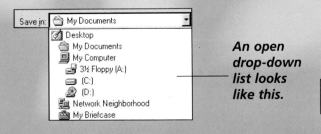

An open drop-down list looks like this.

Tick boxes   Some choices are presented as tick boxes. To select a tick box option, click in its box and a tick will appear. Click in the box again to deselect the option. You can choose as many tick boxes as you like.

This is an example of some tick boxes.

Property sheets   Some dialog boxes are divided into sections called property sheets. Property sheets are like separate pages. Each one has a divider tab at the top. To look at a different property sheet in a dialog box, click on its divider tab.

This dialog box has two property sheets.

Divider tab

Command buttons   Every dialog box has buttons which let you finish your selection. These are called command buttons. Click on a command button to use it.

The most common command buttons you will use are *OK, Cancel* and *Apply,* shown below. *OK* closes the dialog box and puts your choices into effect. *Cancel* closes the dialog box, and ignores any choices you have made. *Apply* puts your choices into effect without closing the dialog box.

These are the most common command buttons.

Typing with WordPad

WordPad is a program which comes with Windows® 98. You can use it to type and organize text, and change the way text looks on a page. This is called word processing.

Open WordPad

A piece of work you produce in a word processing program is called a document. When you open WordPad, a new document opens automatically. To open WordPad, open the Start menu. Point at Programs until its submenu opens, and then point at Accessories until its submenu opens. Click on *WordPad*. The WordPad window, shown below, will open.

This is the WordPad window.

Menu bar   Toolbar   Format bar   Ruler

Status bar   **Page**

WordPad tools

The bars on the WordPad window, shown above, contain tools for working with text. If any of these bars is missing from your WordPad window, open the View menu and click on a bar's name to display it.

Type some text

**Return   Enter
key   key**

To type, click on the page. A small flashing line will appear. This is the cursor. It shows where the text will appear when you type. Try typing text similar to that shown below. When one line is full, the text will flow onto the next line. To start typing on a new line before a line is full, press either the Return key or the Enter key on your keyboard.

This shows some text typed into a WordPad window.

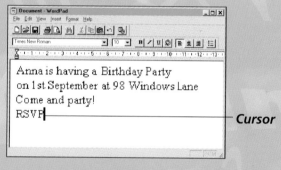

Anna is having a Birthday Party
on 1st September at 98 Windows Lane
Come and party!
RSVP

Cursor

Move the cursor

To move the cursor within the text area, click on the page. The cursor will jump to that position. To move the cursor to a blank part of the page, press the Return key. This will move the cursor down the page line by line.

Delete text

You can erase, or delete, text you have typed. To delete text to the right of the cursor, press the Delete key. To delete text to the left of the cursor, press the Backspace key.

Delete key

Backspace key

Select text

To change a piece of text, you need to highlight, or select, it first. To do this, position your pointer at one end of the text and press your left mouse button down. Drag the pointer to the other end of the text, and let go of the button. The text will be selected, as shown below. To deselect text, click elsewhere on the page.

 The blue part of this text is selected.

Cut and paste

You can move sections of text from one part of a document to another. To do this, select some text, then click on the Cut button shown below. You will find this on the Format bar. The text will disappear. It is stored in a place, not shown on your display, called the Clipboard (see page 36). Position the cursor where you want to move the text to and click on the Paste button. The text will reappear in that position.

The Clipboard can only store one item at a time. Each time you store something new, it replaces what was there before.

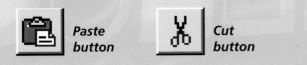

Paste button   **Cut button**

Copy

You can copy a piece of text. To do this, select the text and click on the Copy button, shown here. A copy of the text will be saved onto the Clipboard. You can then paste the copy onto the page.

Copy button

Find and replace

You can find and replace a particular word or phrase wherever it appears in a document. To do this, open the Edit menu and click on *Replace*. A dialog box like the one below will appear.

This is the Replace box.

Replace	? X
Find what:	Find Next
Replace with:	Replace
☐ Match whole word only	Replace All
☐ Match case	Cancel

Type the text you want to find into the *Find what* box. Then type the text you want to replace it with in the *Replace with* box. Click on the *Replace* button. The first piece of matching text in your document will be found and selected. Click on *Replace* again to replace it. The next match will automatically be selected. If you don't want to replace the selected text, click on the *Find Next* button to select the next match.

⚠ Warning

Don't close your document until you have saved it. You will find out how to save what you have done on page 18.

WordPad text styles

WordPad has lots of other tools which allow you to change the way your text looks. For example, you can change the colour, size or appearance of text. This section tells you how to use these tools to add style to your work.

Setting up your page

When a new document is created in WordPad, its size and shape are set for you automatically. However, if you want to, you can change the size and shape of your

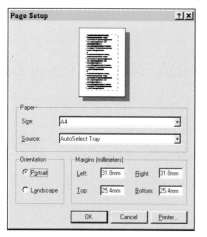

document. To do this, open the File menu and select *Page Setup*. The dialog box shown here will appear.

This is the Page Setup box.

Portrait or landscape?

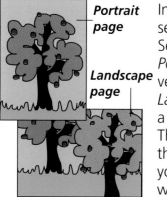

Portrait page

Landscape page

In the *Orientation* section of the Page Setup box, click on *Portrait* to choose a vertical page, or *Landscape* to choose a horizontal page. The example page in the dialog box shows you what the page will look like.

Page size

You can choose what size paper you will want to print your document onto (see page 27). To do this, select a size from the *Size* drop-down list in the *Paper* section of the Page Setup box, and then click on *OK*.

Position text

In a WordPad window, the text you type starts from the left-hand side. This is called aligned to the left. You can make text align to the right, or position it in the middle of the page. To do this, select the text and then click on one of the buttons shown below.

Use these buttons to position your text.

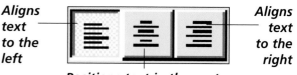

Aligns text to the left

Aligns text to the right

Positions text in the centre

Tabs and rulers

You can use the ruler to position text. If you press the Tab key on your keyboard the cursor will jump a set distance. To change this distance, click on the ruler in several places. L-shaped symbols called tab stops will appear in the places you click. If you press the Tab key, the cursor will jump to the next tab stop. You can use this to line up text. To get rid of a tab stop, drag it off the left-hand side of the ruler.

Tab key

This is a tab stop.

line	text	up
using	tab	stops

Change the style of text

The style of a set of letters and symbols that make up text is called its font. WordPad automatically uses a font called Times New Roman. You can choose from different fonts.

Here are a few examples of different fonts.

Arial
Comic Sans MS
Σψμβολ (Symbol)
▶📠 🐌 ♥①●■? (Webdings™)

To change the font, select a section of text, and select a font from the drop-down list in the Font box. You will find the Font box on your Format bar.

Font box

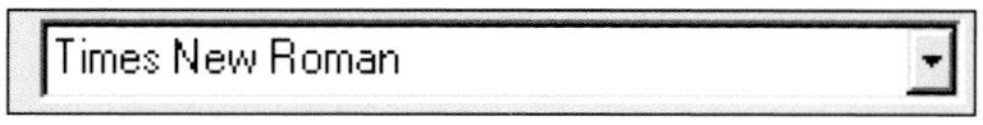

```
Times New Roman              ▼
```

Colouring text

You can change the colour of text. Select the text you want to alter and click on the Color button on the Format bar. Click on a colour on the drop-down list to select it.

Color button

abcde

Change the text size

You can change the size of text. Text sizes are measured in points. WordPad automatically uses a 10 point size. To change the size of your text, select it, then choose a size from the text size box on the Format bar.

These are different text sizes.

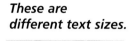
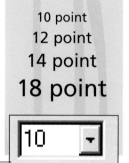

10 point
12 point
14 point
18 point

```
10         ▼
```

This is the text size box.

More style

You can change the look of text by making it **bold**, *italic*, or underlined. To do this, select a section of text and click on one of the buttons shown here. These buttons are on the Format bar. Click on a button again to switch it off.

 Underlines text

 Makes text bold

 Makes text italic

Be creative

Try out the different tools on the WordPad document you created on page 14 to find a style you like. The picture on the right shows the sorts of effects you can achieve.

Various text styles have been used in this document.

Different parts of text are different sizes.

The text is centred.

Anna is having a

Birthday Party

on 1st September **at** 98 Windows Lane

Come and party!
RSVP

This text is bold and under-lined.

Saving your work

Any piece of work you create in a program is called a file. When you have created a file, you can keep it, or save it, for future use. This section tells you how to save your work and also how to open files that you have saved.

Disks

Normally you save a file onto your computer in a place called its hard disk. If you want to save your file to use it on another computer, you can save a copy of it onto a floppy disk. A floppy disk is a plastic disk which you can use in other computers as well as your own.

Floppy disks look like this.

Save a new file

When you save a new file, you need to name it, and choose a place to store the file on your computer. The Save As box, shown below, enables you to do this. To save a file, open the File menu from the Menu bar and click on *Save As*. The dialog box shown below will appear on your display.

This is the Save As box.

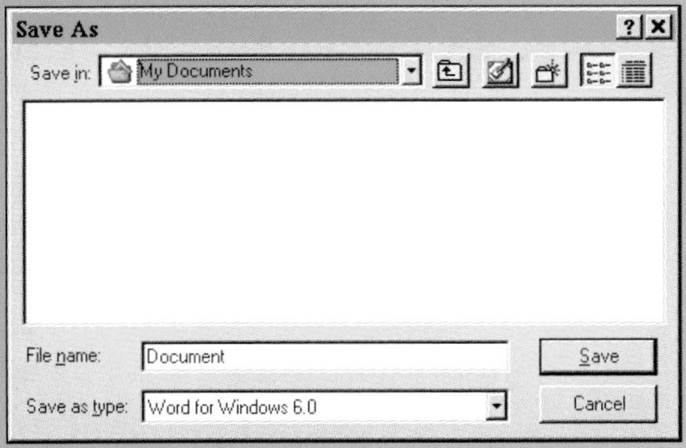

Save As	? X
Save in: My Documents	
File name: Document	Save
Save as type: Word for Windows 6.0	Cancel

Choose a place to save

To select a place to save your file, open the *Save in* drop-down list at the top of the Save As box. The menu contains different icons. Each icon represents a different place on your computer which can store information.

The hard disk of your computer is usually called *C:*. It is divided up into folders (see page 29). One of the folders is called My Documents. This is the best place to save your files. To select it as the place to store your file, click on its icon and *My Documents* will appear in the *Save in* box.

Name and save your file

To name your file, click in the *File name* box of the Save As box. Delete the name that is there and type in a name for your file. It is best to give your file a descriptive name, so that you will remember what it is. For example, you could call the WordPad file created on pages 14 to 17 *Party Invitation*. You can use any name you like, but you cannot use any of these symbols: **/ \ * < > ? " :**

Once you have selected a place and a name for your file, click on the *Save* button to save it.

Save onto a floppy disk

If you want to save a file onto a floppy disk, you must first put a disk into your computer. In the Save As box, select *3½ Floppy [A:]* from the *Save in* drop-down list. Name the file, and click on *Save*. You can then take the floppy disk out of your computer.

Save changes

If you change a file after you have saved it, you need to save it again to store the changes you have made. To do this, open the File menu and select *Save*. The computer will automatically replace the old version of the file with the new version.

Make a copy

If you want to change a file but keep the original version, you can make a copy of it. Save the original file before you make any changes to it. Once it is saved, select *Save As* again. Type in a different name for the file, and click on *Save*. A copy, which you can change, will be saved with that name.

Close your file

When you have finished using a file and have saved it, you can close it. Close the file and the program by clicking on the Close button.

If you try to close a file which has not been saved, a warning box will appear, asking whether you want to save the file. If you do, click on *Yes*. If you have not saved the file at all yet, the *Save As* box will open. Otherwise, it will save over the old version. The file will then close automatically.

The Warning dialog box looks like this.

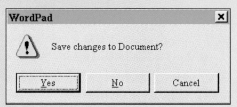

Re-opening a saved file

To re-open a file you have saved in the My Documents folder, open the Start menu, then the Documents submenu, and click on *My Documents*. The My Documents window, shown below, will appear.

The My Documents window

![The My Documents window screenshot]
C:\My Documents — File Edit View Go Favorites Help — Back Forward Up — Address C:\My Documents — My Documents — Party Invitation — Select an item to view its description. — 16 object(s) (plus 1 hidden) — 1.71MB — My Computer

This is the file you saved.   **View area**

In the View area, you can see all the files you have stored in the My Documents folder. Double-click on the icon of the file you want to open.

Open a file in a program

There is another way to open a file you have saved. This is the best way to open a WordPad document if you have another word processing program (such as Microsoft® Word) on your computer. First, open the program in which the file was created. In the program's window, open the File menu and select *Open*. A dialog box will appear, showing the contents of the My Documents folder. Select the icon of the file you want to open and click on the *Open* button.

Pictures with Paint

Paint is a program which is included in Windows® 98. You can use it to create your own pictures and designs.

The Paint window

To open Paint, open the Start menu, then the Accessories submenu and click on *Paint*. The Paint window, shown below, will appear.

This is the Paint window.

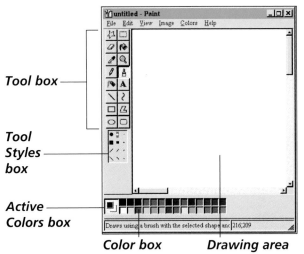

Tool box

Tool Styles box

Active Colors box

Color box   Drawing area

Drawing tools

To draw, first click on either the Pencil tool or the Brush tool (shown below) in the Tool box. Then drag on the drawing area with your mouse to draw lines. If you click on the Brush tool, some options will appear in the Tool Styles box. They show different shapes of brush stroke you can choose from. Click on one of these to use it.

These are the drawing tools.

Pencil tool

Brush tool

Brush strokes in the Tool Styles box.

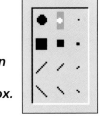

Drawing in colour

You can draw in colour. To do this, click on the Pencil or the Brush tool, then click on a colour in the Color box. The colour you select will appear in the Active Colors box, shown below. Drag your mouse on the drawing area to draw using the colour.

This is the Active Colors box.

The colour you ——— select appears here.

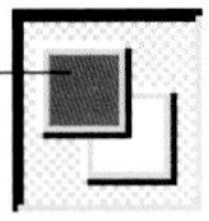

Filling and spraying colour

You can colour in an area using the Fill tool, shown below. To do this, click on the Fill tool. Then select a colour and click on an enclosed area to fill it with the colour.

You can create a spray can effect using the Airbrush tool, shown below. To do this, select the Airbrush tool, click on a colour and then drag your mouse on the drawing area. Choose how much colour is sprayed at a time by selecting an option from the Tool Styles box.

Fill tool

Airbrush tool

Erasing

You can erase parts of your drawing using the Eraser tool. To use it, click on the tool and then drag the pointer over the area you want to erase. The area will turn white. You can choose from different sizes of eraser in the Tool Styles box.

Eraser tool

If you want to erase everything in the drawing area and begin again, open the Image menu and click on *Clear Image*.

Tip: Undo mistakes

If you make a mistake you can undo it by selecting *Undo* from the Edit menu. You can undo the last three things you did.

Drawing shapes

You can draw shapes using the tools shown below. To draw a shape, click on a tool and then drag your mouse on the drawing area. Drag the shape to the size you want before releasing the button. To draw a shape in a colour, select the colour before drawing.

You can use these tools to draw shapes, like the ones shown here.

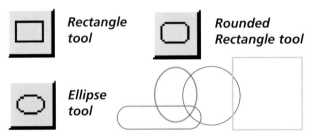

Rectangle tool

Rounded Rectangle tool

Ellipse tool

You can use the Polygon tool, shown below, to draw a many-sided shape. It works differently from the other shape tools. To use this tool, first select it. Then drag your mouse on the drawing area, and release the mouse button to draw one side of your shape. Drag to draw more sides in the same way. To finish the shape, join the last side to the starting point.

The Polygon tool enables you to draw many-sided shapes, like these.

Polygon tool

Drawing lines

There are two tools you can use to draw lines, shown below. The Line tool draws a straight line. To use it, drag out a line on the drawing area. Release the mouse button to end the line. The Curve tool draws a wavy line. To use it, drag out a straight line. Then create curves in the line by dragging it in two places.

Line tool

Curve tool

Start painting

Try using some of these tools to create your own picture. Draw a picture to go with the WordPad document you created on pages 14 to 17. Name it *Party Picture* and save it in the My Documents folder (see page 18). Find out how to put the text and the picture together on page 24.

This picture was created in Paint. The labels show which tools were used to create different effects.

Brush (flat brush stroke)   Polygon   Brush (round brush stroke)

Pencil   Fill

Paint tricks and tips

There are some tools and techniques in Paint which can come in handy when you are creating a picture. You can use them to create some fun effects.

Enlarge the drawing area

In the Paint window, there are eight tiny blue dots around the edges of the drawing area. You can't draw outside of the area enclosed by these dots, but you can change the size of drawing area. Maximize the Paint window, then position your pointer over the bottom, right-hand dot. Your pointer symbol will turn into a double arrow. Drag the dot to change the size of the drawing area.

Drag to make the drawing area bigger.

Cut out part of your picture

You can cut out and move parts of a picture. Use the Select tool to cut out a rectangular area. Click on the tool, then drag a rectangle around the area you want to cut out. You can move the cut-out section by dragging it to a new position. Once you click outside the cut-out section, it will be fixed in position on your display. The Free-Form Select tool enables you to cut out an area which is not rectangular. Click on it and then drag a line around an area to cut it out.

 Select

 Free-Form Select

Copy an image

You can make copies of an image you have drawn. To do this, cut out the image, using either the Select tool, or the Free-Form Select tool. Hold down the *Ctrl* key on your keyboard and drag the image to a new position. A copy of the image will be left in the original position.

This shows a sunflower being copied to make a row of flowers.

Make trails

You can make an image leave a trail as you drag it. To do this, cut out an image using the Select tool. In the Tool Styles box, click on the bottom Tool Styles option. Then hold down the Shift key on your keyboard and drag the image. It will leave a trail behind it.

Shift key

The picture below was made by drawing a bird like the one on the left, and then dragging it to create a trail.

Flip and rotate images

You can turn images over and around in Paint. To do this, first cut the image out using the Select tool. Then, open the Image menu and click on *Flip/Rotate*. A dialog box will appear. The pictures below show some effects you can achieve if you select different options from the dialog box.

Rotate by angle (90°)
This option revolves the image by 90°.

Flip horizontal
This turns the image over from left to right.

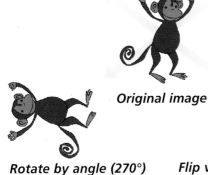

Original image

Rotate by angle (270°)
This revolves the image by 270°.

Flip vertical
This turns the image over top to bottom.

Stretch or shrink an image

You can stretch or shrink an image. To do this, first cut out the image using the Select tool. Then open the Image menu and click on *Stretch/Skew*. In the dialog box that appears, type in how much you want to stretch or shrink the image by in the *Horizontal* and *Vertical* sections. To make the image bigger, type in a number higher than 100%. To make it smaller, type a number lower than 100%.

More colours ⓬

There are more colours to choose from than those displayed in the Paint window. To choose another colour, open the Color menu and select *Edit Colors*. The Edit Colors box, shown below, will open. Click on a colour from the *Basic colors* palette, and then click on *OK*. The colour will replace your selected colour in the Active Colors box.

This is the Edit Colors dialog box.

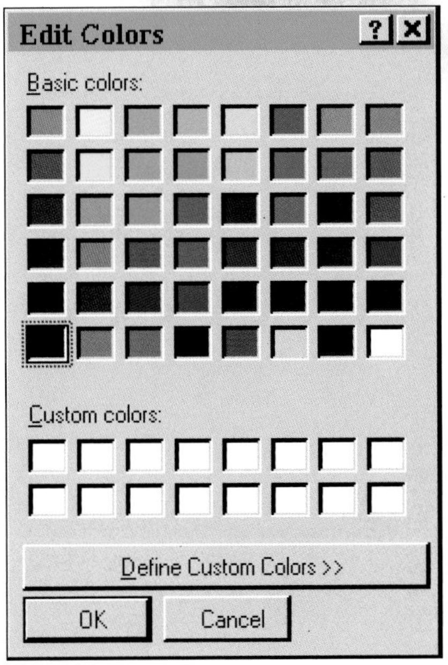

Invert colours

You can swap all the colours in your picture for their opposites. To do this, open the Image menu and select *Invert Colors*. Select this option again to turn the colours back.

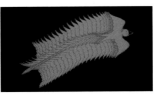

The bird image looks like this when you invert its colours.

Combining words and pictures

In Windows® 98, there are different ways in which you can put words and pictures together. This section shows you three different ways of doing this.

Add text in Paint

In Paint you can add text to a picture. To do this, click on the Text tool, shown below. Before you can type, you need to make a box to type in. Click on the drawing area and drag out a box. This is a text box. A cursor will appear inside it. You can then type into the text box. You can drag the edges of the box to change its size.

Text tool

A text box

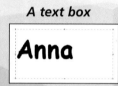

When you draw a text box the Text Toolbar appears. Use it to select the font, text size and style. If the Toolbar does not appear automatically, open the View menu and click on its name.

This is the Text Toolbar.

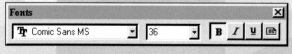

Paint text

When you have finished typing, click on the drawing area outside the text box. When you do this, the text becomes part of your picture. You could try decorating it.

This text was made in the program Paint.

About objects

You can insert a file created in one program into a file created in another. For example, you can insert a Paint file into a WordPad file. When one file is inserted into another, the inserted file is called an object.

Paste an object into a file

An easy way to place one file into another file is to copy and paste it. For example, you can paste *Party Picture,* created in Paint (see page 21) into *Party Invitation,* created in WordPad (see pages 14 to 17).

To do this, first open the Paint picture you created called *Party Picture.* It is in the My Documents folder. Use the Select tool to cut out the picture. When the picture has a box around it, it is selected. You can now copy it by opening the Edit menu and selecting *Copy.* A copy of the selected picture is saved onto the Clipboard, ready to be pasted. Then click on the Close button to close the Paint window.

The blue dotted line around the picture shows that it is selected.

Next, open the WordPad file *Party Invitation* from the My Documents folder. Position your cursor on the page in the place that you want the picture to appear. To paste the picture into the document, open the Edit menu and select *Paste.* The picture will appear in the document.

Insert an object into a file

There is another way to insert an object into a file. Open the file into which you want to insert an object. Open the Insert menu and select *Object*. In the Insert Object box that appears, select *Create from File*. Then click on the *Browse* button.

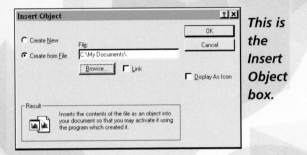

This is the Insert Object box.

The Browse box, shown below, will open. It contains all the folders and files that are stored on your computer. *My Documents* appears automatically in the *Look in* box, Its contents are shown in the view area. Double-click on the file you want to insert, then click on *OK* in the Insert Object box.

This is the Browse box.

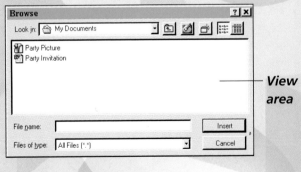

View area

Save

Remember to save the file with the object inserted into it. Open the File menu and select *Save As.* Give it a name and save it in the My Documents folder.

Change an object

You can change an object which has been inserted into a file. If you click on the object, a box with handles (shown below) will appear around it. You can change the shape of the object by dragging the handles. You can move the object by dragging it to a new position. You can also delete it, as you would text, by using the Delete key.

This is a framed object.

A handle

If you double-click on an object, it will open in the program in which it was created. You can change the file using this program. When you have changed the file, save it and click on the program's Close button. The changes will show on the inserted object.

This shows a WordPad file (Party Invitation) with a Paint file (Party Picture) inserted into it.

Anna is having a

Birthday Party

on 1st September at 98 Windows Lane

Come and party!

RSVP

Photos on your computer

You can transfer photos and other pictures onto your computer using a program called Imaging for Windows®. You will need a scanner or a digital camera. These convert pictures into a form that your computer can display.

Scan in a picture

To transfer a picture onto your computer using a scanner, first make sure the scanner is connected to your computer. Next, open Imaging for Windows®. To do this, open the Start menu, the Programs submenu then the Accessories submenu, and click on *Imaging.* Put your picture into the scanner and click on the Scan New button (shown below). In the dialog box that appears, click on the scan option. After a short time, the picture will appear in the Imaging window.

This is the Imaging window.

Scan New button

This photo was scanned in.

Tip: Scanner and camera

If you have a digital camera and a scanner, you need to tell your computer which to use. Open the File menu and click on *Select Scanner.* In the dialog box, select the device you want to use and click on *OK.*

Digital cameras

A digital camera is like a normal camera, but instead of developing the photographs you take with it, you can transfer them onto your computer to look at or print onto paper (see page 27).

When you have taken some photos, connect the camera to your computer. In the Imaging window, click on the Scan New button. The dialog box that appears depends on the type of camera you have. Select the option which enables you to get a photo from the camera. The photo will appear in the Imaging window.

Be creative with pictures

Once you have transferred a picture onto your computer, save it into your My Documents folder. You can then use it in lots of creative ways. For example, you can paste a photo into a WordPad file. To do this, open the Edit menu in the Imaging window and select *Copy Page.* Then open the WordPad file, open its Edit menu and select *Paste.* The photo will appear in the WordPad window.

This shows a letter with a photo pasted into it.

This photo was pasted into Paint and drawn on using Paint tools.

Printing

When you have created a file, you can print a copy of it onto paper. Before you do this, make sure your printer is attached to your computer, switched on, and has paper loaded into it.

Print Preview

Before you can print a file, you need to open it. You can check how the file will look on paper before printing it. To do this, open the File menu and select *Print Preview*. A window like the one shown below will open to show how your file will look on paper.

If your file is longer than a page, click on the *Two Page* button to see both pages at once. To get back to the main program window, click on the *Close* button in the Print Preview box. You can then make changes to your file before printing it.

This is the Print Preview box, showing how a letter will look when printed.

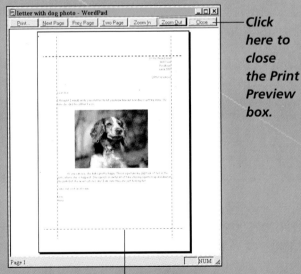

Click here to close the Print Preview box.

The dotted line shows where the margins are.

Print your file

Once you like the way your file looks, open the File menu and click on *Print*. The Print dialog box, shown below, will appear.

This is the Print dialog box.

The name of your printer will appear here.

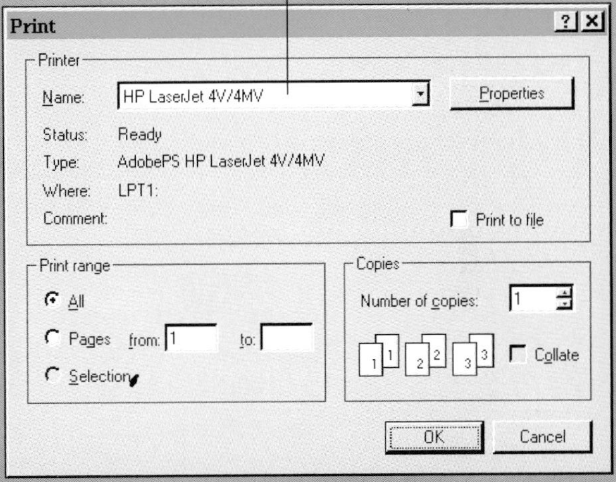

If you only want to print certain pages of a file, select *Pages* in the *Print range* section of the dialog box. Type the number of the first page you want to print in the *from* box and the last page in the *to* box. Then type in the number of copies you want in the *Number of copies* box in the *Copies* section.

Click on the *Properties* button to see more print options. In the *Paper size* section of this box, you can choose the size of paper you want to print onto. Choose between a portrait and landscape page layout in the *Orientation* section. Click on OK when you have finished.

Depending on what kind of printer you have, the Print box will either have a *Print* button or an OK button. Click on it to print your file.

What's on My Computer?

My Computer is a program which enables you to look at places, or locations, on your computer in which files and other types of information are stored.

Open My Computer

To open My Computer, double-click on its icon on your desktop. The My Computer window, shown below, will open. The icons in the View area stand for locations on your computer in which information is stored.

My Computer

This is the My Computer window.

View area

Disks and drives

Your computer stores information in locations called disks. The disk inside your computer is called a hard disk. There are also disks which you can put into and take out of your computer, such as floppy disks and CD-ROMs (see page 46).

Each disk is contained or inserted into a location on your computer called a drive. Usually, the hard disk drive is called *C:*. Each disk drive has its own icon, shown below.

Disk drive icons

Hard disk drive   **CD-ROM drive**   **Floppy disk drive**

View options

You can change the way the contents of the My Computer window are displayed. You can view them as large icons, small icons, in a list, or with details about each item. To choose a different display option, open the View menu and select an option. The My Computer window shown on the left has *Large Icons* selected.

These are the display options.

3½ Floppy (A:)	
(D:)	
(C:)	
Printers	
Control Panel	**List**

3½ Floppy (A:)	3½ Inch Floppy Disk
(D:)	CD-ROM Disc
(C:)	Local Disk
Printers	System Folder
Control Panel	System Folder

Details

Small icons

3½ Floppy (A:)	(D:)	(C:)
Printers	Control Panel	

Browsing

You can look at information in different locations on your computer by double-clicking on icons in the My Computer window. This is called browsing. There are two ways of browsing. You can either look at each location in a separate window, or the single window can change to show each location.

Single window browsing

To use this book, you need to set your computer to browse using a single window. To do this, open the View menu and select *Folder Options*. On the General property sheet, click on the *Custom* option, then click on *Settings*. Select *Open each folder in the same window* and click on *OK*. Close the Folder Options box.

Finding your way around

To see what is stored on your hard disk, double-click on the hard disk icon. The view area of the My Computer window will change to show the contents of the hard disk. The name on the Title bar also changes to the name of the location being displayed.

The My Computer window showing the contents of the hard disk

— Title bar

— Folders

— View area

Folders and files

The hard disk contains files and folders. A folder, like the My Documents folder, is a location where you can store files. Folders can also contain other folders called subfolders.

To see the contents of a folder or subfolder, double-click on its icon. If you double-click on a file, it will open in a separate window. Try opening a file you have saved.

This is the My Computer window showing the contents of the My Documents folder.

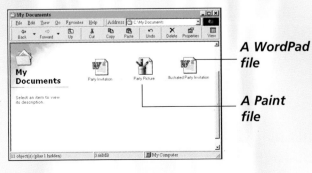

— A WordPad file

— A Paint file

Browsing tools 98

There are tools on the My Computer Toolbar which can help you to browse.

The *Back* and *Forward* buttons enable you to retrace your steps when browsing. You can look at places you have already looked at, by clicking on *Back*. You can then click on *Forward* to get to where you were again.

Click on the *Up* button to display the next location up from the one being shown. For example, if you are looking at the contents of the My Documents folder, click on *Up* to show the contents of the hard drive, where My Documents is stored. Click on *Up* again to show the contents of My Computer.

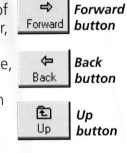

Forward button

Back button

Up button

Address bar 98

The Address bar displays the location, or address, of the folder you are looking at. For example, if you are looking at the My Documents folder, the address will be *C:\My Documents*. This shows that My Documents is stored on the hard disk (*C:*).

You can use the Address bar to look at different locations on your computer. Select an address from the drop-down list. The window will change to show the contents of that location.

This is the Address bar.

Organizing your files

Windows Explorer, like My Computer, is a program which you can use to look at the information stored on your computer. You can also use it to organize your files.

Open Windows Explorer

You can open Windows Explorer from the Start menu. Open the Start menu, then the Programs submenu, and click on *Windows Explorer*. A window like the one shown below will open on your display.

This is the Windows Explorer window.

Browsing tools 98

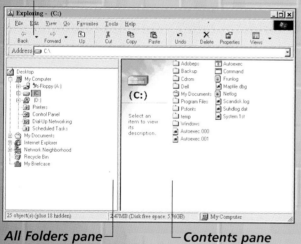

All Folders pane ⎤   ⎣ **Contents pane**

Explore using two panes

The Windows Explorer window has two panes, shown above. If you click on an item in the All Folders pane, its contents will be shown in the Contents pane. By doing this, you can use the All Folders pane to find your way to different locations on your computer, and the Contents pane to look at the information that is stored there.

All Folders pane

The All Folders pane displays the different locations on your computer in a list of icons like the one shown below. The lines, or branches, connecting the icons together show where each item is stored. For example, the hard disk icon (shown as *C:* here) has branches leading to folders, including the My Documents folder. This shows that these folders are stored on the hard disk.

This shows the branches connecting icons together.

Plus and minus signs

A plus sign (+) by an icon means it contains other locations. If you click on the plus sign, branches will appear, leading from the icon, to show these locations. When you click on a plus sign it becomes a minus sign (-). Click on this to hide the branches again. If an icon doesn't have a sign beside it, then it doesn't contain folders or disks. It may still contain files, which will be shown in the Contents pane.

Contents pane

The Contents pane works in a similar way to the My Computer window. You can browse in this pane without using the All Folders pane. Browse in the Contents pane by double-clicking on icons, or using the Browsing tools on the Toolbar.

Create a new folder

Windows Explorer enables you to organize your files. You can create subfolders in the My Documents folder and then organize your files into groups. To do this, first click on *My Documents* in the All Folders pane. Next, open the File menu, then the New submenu, and click on *Folder*. A new folder icon will appear in the Contents pane.

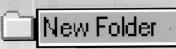

This is a new folder icon.

Give your subfolder a name that describes what will be stored in it. To do this, type a name into the box that is selected, and press the Return key on your keyboard. For example, name this subfolder *Party* and keep your party invitation files in it.

Moving files

You can move a file to a different folder by dragging it (see page 7). To do this, make sure you can see the file you want to move in the Contents pane, and the folder you want to move it to in the All Folders pane. Then drag the file to the folder. When the folder is highlighted, release the mouse button to drop the file into the folder.

This shows a file being dragged into a folder.

No entry

If you see this symbol as you are dragging a file, it means you cannot drop the file in that place.

Copy a file

You can make a copy of a file. To do this, drag the file to a new location, holding down the right mouse button instead of the left one. When you release the mouse button, select *Copy Here* from the context menu that appears. You could also copy a file onto a floppy disk in this way.

When copying a file it is a good idea to rename the copy (see below), so that you can tell which file is which.

Rename your folders and files

You can change the name of a folder or a file. To do so, right-click on the folder or file. Select *Rename* from the context menu that appears. The name of the folder or file will be highlighted. Type in a new name for the folder and press the Return key.

Part
con
nois
gam

Explore
Open
Find...
Scan for Viruses
Sharing...
Send To ▶
Cut
Copy
Paste
Create Shortcut
Delete
Rename
Properties

Right-click on a file or folder to show this context menu.

⚠ Warning

Do not move, rename or copy any folder or file which you did not create yourself. Doing so could stop your computer from working.

Multitasking and the Taskbar

In Windows® 98, you can work with more than one window at a time. This is called multitasking. The Taskbar, which is the bar running along the bottom edge of your desktop (shown below), is a useful tool for controlling the windows you are working with on your display.

Program buttons

For each program you open, a button representing that program, called a program button, appears on the Taskbar (see the Taskbar shown below).

You can click on a program button to minimize an open window, if you want to move it out of the way. If a window is minimized, you can click on its program button to restore the window to its previous size and position on your desktop.

Show the desktop 98

If you have a few windows open on your display but you want to be able to see your desktop, you can minimize all of the windows at once. To do this, click on the Show Desktop icon on the Quick Launch bar (see below). You can click on the icon again to restore the windows to their previous positions on your display.

Active windows

A window you are using is called an active window. Only one window can be active at a time, even though more than one can be open on the desktop.

When a window is active, its program button on the Taskbar is paler than the other buttons and looks as if it has been pushed in. Also, the Title bar of an active window is a different colour from those on other, inactive, windows.

The Solitaire window (see page 39) is active on this desktop. The other windows are inactive.

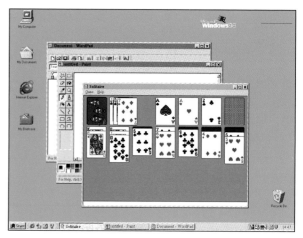

Using windows

If you have a few windows open at once, they may overlap on your desktop. If the window you want to use is hidden by others, click on its program button on the Taskbar. The window will move to the top of the pile of open windows, ready to use.

This is the Taskbar.

Quick Launch bar 98   *Show Desktop icon*   *Program button (active)*   *Program button (inactive)*

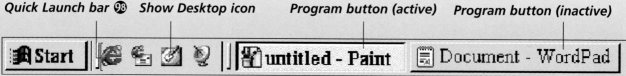

Arranging windows

If you have several windows open at once, you can arrange them on your desktop using the Taskbar. Right-click on a blank part of the Taskbar. From the context menu that appears, select one of the options illustrated below to arrange the windows on your desktop. You can still move windows around on your desktop after arranging them.

Here are the different ways in which you can arrange windows on your desktop.

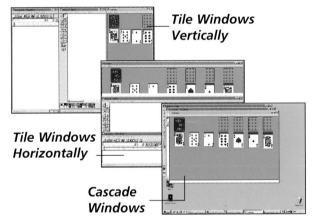

Tile Windows Vertically

Tile Windows Horizontally

Cascade Windows

More room on the Taskbar

If you have lots of windows open at once, the buttons on your Taskbar may become overcrowded, so that you can't read the program names on them. You can make the Taskbar bigger to give the buttons more room. To do this, point at the inside edge of the Taskbar, until your pointer symbol changes to a double-sided arrow. Drag the edge of the Taskbar upwards to make it wider. The buttons will spread out.

Move the Taskbar

You can move the Taskbar to a new position on your desktop. To do this, position your pointer over a blank part of the Taskbar and then drag it to a different side of the desktop. It will jump to the new position.

Tip: Lost your Taskbar?

If you can't see your Taskbar, hold down the Ctrl key on your keyboard and press the Esc key to make it reappear.

Taskbar on top

The Taskbar is a useful tool, which you may need to use at any time. You can set it so that it will never be covered by any open windows on your desktop. Right-click on the Taskbar, select *Properties*, and make sure the option marked *Always on top* is selected.

Hide the Taskbar

You can also set the Taskbar so that it is hidden until you need to use it. To do this, right-click on the Taskbar and select *Properties* from the context menu that appears. Select the *Auto hide* tick box option and click on *OK*.

Click on your desktop and the Taskbar will disappear. It will only pop up again when you move the pointer to the edge of the desktop where it was positioned.

14:27

Finding files

If you forget where you have stored a file or folder on your computer, you can use a program called Find to help you look for it.

Find files or folders

To search for a filè or a folder, open the Start menu, and then the Find submenu. The Find submenu contains options which enable you to search for different types of information. Click on *Files or Folders*, and the dialog box shown below will open.

The Find: All Files box 98

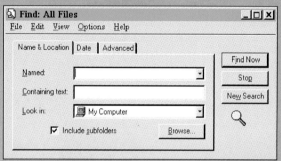

Search by name or location 98

To start a search, you need to give your computer some information about the file or folder you are trying to find.

If you can remember the file's name, or part of its name, type this into the *Named* box on the Name and Location property sheet. If you can remember any unusual words which the lost file contained, you can type them into  the *Containing text* box. Next, tell your computer where to look for the file or folder by selecting a location, such as the hard drive, from the *Look in* drop-down list.

Begin searching

To begin the search, click on the *Find Now* button. Your computer will find any files which match the information you gave and list them in the Find dialog box.

Search by date

You can use the Date property sheet to search for a file according to when it was created or last used.

Select *Find all files*. To specify when a file was made, last changed, or last used, select *Created*, *Modified*, or *Last Accessed* from the drop-down list. Then select approximately when you think you changed, made or used the file by clicking on the radio buttons and arrowheads in the relevant sections.

This is the Date property sheet of the Find: All Files box.

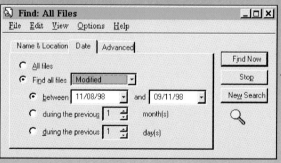

Open or move a found file

When you find a file, you can open it from the Find box by double-clicking on its icon.

If you want to move the file to a new location, so that you will be able to find it more easily, open the Windows Explorer window. Drag the file from the Find window to a new location in the All Folders pane of Windows Explorer.

Deleting files

Each file stored on your computer takes up some storage space. Your hard disk has room for lots of files before it gets full. However, you can avoid using up too much storage space on your computer by deleting files you don't need any more. A program called the Recycle Bin enables you to do this.

Using the Recycle Bin

You can delete files or folders from their location in Windows Explorer, My Computer, or even the Find box. To do this, first make sure you can see the Recycle Bin icon (shown below) on your desktop. Next, make sure you can see the file you want to delete in the Windows Explorer or My Computer window. Then drag the file or folder to the Recycle Bin. When the Recycle Bin icon is highlighted, drop the file or folder into it. A dialog box will appear, asking whether you are sure you want to send this item to the Recycle Bin. Check that the file named in the box is the one you want to delete, and then click on *Yes*. When you have put something in the Recycle Bin, the icon changes from an empty bin to a full one.

The Recycle Bin icon changes when you put something in it.

Delete using a context menu

You can also put a file into the Recycle Bin by right-clicking on it and selecting *Delete* from the menu that appears. Click on *Yes* in the dialog box and the item will be deleted.

Delete by mistake?

If you put something in the Recycle Bin by mistake, don't worry; you can get it back. To do this, first open the Recycle Bin by double-clicking on its icon on the desktop. In the window that appears, right-click on the file or folder you want to retrieve. From the context menu that opens, select *Restore*. The file will disappear from the Recycle Bin window. It will reappear in the place it was originally stored on your hard disk.

You can also retrieve a file or folder by dragging it from the Recycle Bin window to a place in the Windows Explorer or My Computer window.

Empty the Recycle Bin

Files that have been put into the Recycle Bin are being stored, ready to be deleted. They still take up space on your computer. To delete them from your computer altogether, open the Recycle Bin. Open the File menu and select *Empty Recycle Bin*.

A dialog box will appear, asking whether you are sure you want to delete these items. Check that you do not want to keep any of the files. If there are folders, remember to check that you don't want any of the files they contain. Then click on *Yes,* and everything in the Recycle Bin will be deleted for good.

⚠ Warning

Don't delete files or folders which you did not create yourself. It could stop your computer from working.

Handy gadgets

There are some programs included in Windows® 98, which can be handy gadgets to use for particular tasks. Here are a few of them.

Calculator

Windows® 98 has a calculator. To open it, open the Start menu, the Programs submenu, and the Accessories submenu. Click on *Calculator*. A picture of a calculator, shown below, will appear on your display. To use it, click on the buttons.

This is the Standard calculator.

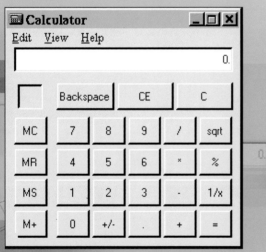

You can choose between a standard or a scientific calculator. A scientific calculator has more buttons which can be used for more complex calculations. To select a calculator, open the View menu and click on its name. If you don't know what a button on the calculator is for, right-click on it, then click on the words *What's this?* An explanation will appear in a box. Click outside the box to close it.

Notepad

Windows® 98 includes a program called Notepad. Notepad is a word processing program, like WordPad. To open Notepad, open the Start menu, the Programs submenu, and then the Accessories submenu. Click on *Notepad*. The Notepad window, shown below, will open.

Notepad has fewer tools than WordPad, but the program opens very quickly. This makes it handy for jotting down notes. Notepad includes a tool you can use to date a document. Open the Edit menu and click on *Time/Date*. The time and date will appear on the page next to the cursor.

This is the Notepad window.

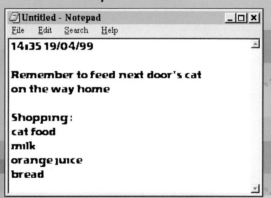

Clipboard Viewer

A program called Clipboard Viewer lets you see what is stored on the Clipboard (see page 15). To open it, open the Start menu, the Programs submenu, the Accessories submenu, and then the System Tools submenu. Click on *Clipboard Viewer*.

When the program opens, whatever is currently stored on the Clipboard will be displayed in the window. You cannot change items within Clipboard Viewer.

Character Map

All the symbols you type, including letters and numbers, are called characters. If you want to use a character which is not on your keyboard, you can add it using a program called Character Map. For example, if you are typing French words you may want to add letters with accents, such as é, è or ê.

To open the Character Map, open the Start menu, the Programs submenu, the Accessories submenu and then click on *Character Map*.

This is the Character Map.

Select a font here.

The character you select will appear here.

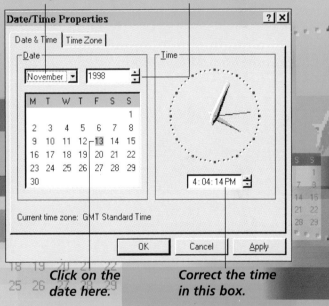

This area shows a range of different characters you can use.

To use the Character Map, select the font you want to use from the *Font* drop-down list. Different fonts have different characters available, which are displayed in the grid area. Click on a character, for example é, in the grid area, and then click on the *Select* button. The character will appear in the *Characters to copy* box. Click on *Copy* to copy the character onto the Clipboard. You can then paste the character into a file.

The clock

The clock is displayed in the System Tray on the Taskbar. If you point at it, a little box will appear, showing the date.

If the time or date is incorrect, you can alter it. To do this, double-click on the clock. The Date/Time Properties box will open. Select the correct time and date in the relevant boxes, as shown in the picture below, then click on the *OK* button.

This is the Date/Time Properties box.

Select the month from the drop-down menu.

Click on the arrowheads to select the year.

Click on the date here.

Correct the time in this box.

Tip: Keeping time

Your computer keeps time even when it is switched off. It is important to set the right time, as your computer keeps track of when files are created or used. You can set your computer to run certain programs at specific times (see page 73).

Games

There are four games included in Windows® 98. This section introduces these games and explains how to use the instructions in the games to learn how to play them.

To open a game, open the Programs submenu, then open the Accessories submenu. On the Games submenu, click on the name of a game. The game will open in a window on your display.

How to play

Each game has instructions and tips on how to play. To read them, open the game's Help menu and click on *Help Topics*. The Help window, shown below, will open.

The topics that you can find out about are listed in the left-hand pane of the window. On the Contents property sheet, click on a topic to show its explanation in the right-hand pane. Some text in the right-hand pane is underlined. If you click on it, a box will appear, containing an explanation of the underlined text. Click elsewhere in the Help window to close this box. The Help window is part of the Windows® 98 Help system (see page 74).

This is the FreeCell game Help window.

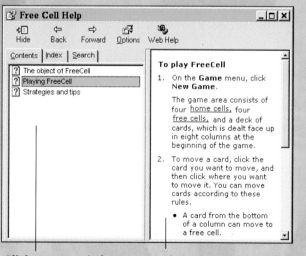

Click on a topic here.   Read the instructions here.

Minesweeper

Minesweeper is a game for one player. When you open the program, a new game is ready for you to play.

The aim is to mark hidden mines with flags without uncovering any of them. Click on a square to uncover it. Some of the uncovered squares contain numbers, which tell you how many mines are hidden in the eight squares that surround that one. Right-click on a square to mark it with a flag if you think there's a mine there. Click on the smiley face to start a new game.

This is a game of Minesweeper.

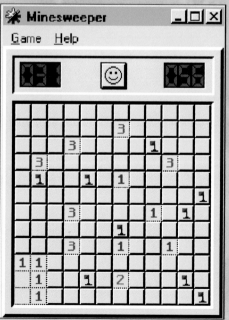

FreeCell

FreeCell is a card game for one player. To begin a game, open the program, then open the Game menu and select *New Game*. Cards will appear in the window.

The aim is to end up with all the cards in piles of different suits in the Home cells (see picture). To begin with, the cards are dealt into rows in a random order by the computer. You have to move the cards between the rows to get them in descending order, so they can be moved into the Home cells. There are rules about how you are allowed to move the cards. A FreeCell game is shown here.

This shows a FreeCell game in mid-play.

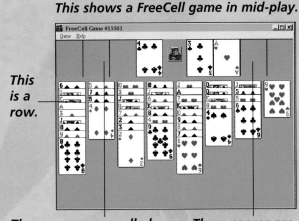

This is a row.

These spaces are called Free cells.

These spaces are the Home cells.

Solitaire

Solitaire is a card game for one player. To start, open the Game menu and select *Deal*.

The aim is to end up with all the cards in piles of different suits in the Home spaces (see picture). To start, the cards are in rows, like in FreeCell. Some cards are face-down beneath others. You can only look at these after moving the cards on top. You can use cards from the pack throughout the game.

A Solitaire game in mid-play looks like this.

Pack of cards   A row   Home spaces

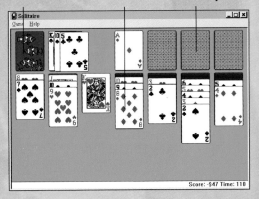

Hearts

This is a card game for four players. You can play it with other people, using computers connected to yours, or against your computer.

When you open Hearts, a dialog box appears. Type your name into it. To play against your computer, select *I want to be dealer*. Click on *OK*, and then press the F2 key on your keyboard to start the game.

The aim is to end up with the lowest score. All Hearts and the Queen of Spades are the scoring cards. You have to try to get rid of these cards during the game.

This game of Hearts is being played by Anna against the computer's three imaginary players.

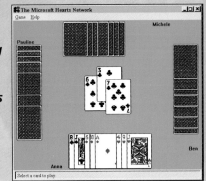

Decorating your display

The colours and fonts used on your display - on menus, windows and the desktop - are called display settings. You can change your display settings to give your computer a personalized look. Windows® 98 has lots of different colours, fonts and patterns which you can choose from. You can also decorate your display according to a theme (see page 42).

Open Display Properties

To change your display settings, use the Display Properties box. To open it, right-click on your desktop and select *Properties* on the menu that appears. The Display Properties box, shown below, will appear. It has property sheets which you can use to change different parts of your display. There is an example display in the dialog box, which shows what the settings you choose will look like.

This shows the Background property sheet in the Display Properties box.

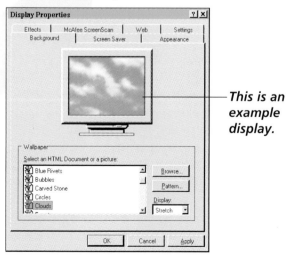

This is an example display.

Wallpaper your desktop

You can put a picture or pattern onto your desktop, beneath your icons. This is called wallpaper. There are various wallpaper designs you can choose from to brighten up your display.

To choose a design, use the Background property sheet in the Display Properties box. Select a design from the *Wallpaper* list. The example display will change to show what the design looks like. In the *Display* box you can choose how to display the wallpaper: *Tile* repeats the wallpaper design across the desktop, *Center* puts it in the middle of the desktop, and *Stretch* enlarges the design to fill the desktop. Click on the *Apply* button to put the wallpaper onto your desktop.

These are two of the different wallpaper designs in Windows® 98.

Forest

Clouds

Tip: Design some wallpaper

You can design your own wallpaper using Paint. First open Paint, create and save a design. Then open the Paint File menu, and select *Set As Wallpaper (Centered)* or *Set as Wallpaper (Tiled)* to put your design onto your desktop.

Screen savers

If a display stays the same for too long, it can leave a permanent mark on the screen. A screen saver is a moving design which prevents this from happening. A screen saver appears automatically

when your computer display hasn't been used for a certain length of time. When you want to use your display again, just move your mouse. The screen saver will disappear.

Choose a screen saver

Windows® 98 has some fun screen savers you can use. To choose one, use the Screen Saver property sheet in the Display Properties box. Select a design from the drop-down list. Click on the *Preview* button to see what it looks like.

You can change parts of some screen savers, such as their colour. To do this, click on the *Settings* button in the *Screen Saver* section. A dialog box will appear, offering choices about the selected screen saver.

You can use the *Wait* box to choose how long your computer should wait before starting the screen saver. Click on the *Apply* button to use the selected screen saver.

Here are two Windows® 98 screen savers.

3D Flower Box

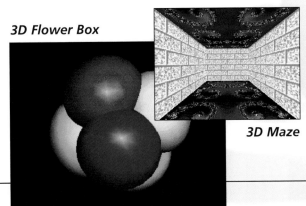

3D Maze

Change the display scheme

You can change the colours and fonts used on windows and menus. To do this, use the Appearance property sheet in the Display Properties box. From the *Scheme* drop-down list, select a display scheme. This changes all the fonts and colours at the same time. The example display shows how the scheme will look. Click on *Apply* to use it.

This shows the Appearance property sheet.

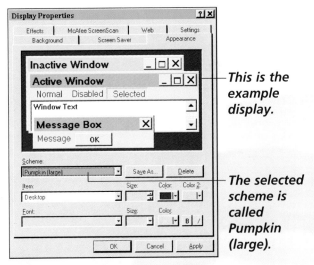

This is the example display.

The selected scheme is called Pumpkin (large).

Design your own scheme

You can change individual parts of your display, using the Appearance property sheet (see above). Click on a part of the display shown in the example display. Its name will appear in the *Item* box. Then, to change the colour used on this part of the display, select a colour from the *Color* drop-down list. To change the font used for the text, select one from the *Font* drop-down list.

You can save your own display scheme by clicking on the *Save As* button. Type in a name for your scheme, and click on OK. It will be saved onto the *Scheme* drop-down list.

Desktop Themes 98

You can liven up your display with a Windows® 98 feature called Desktop Themes. A theme changes all of your computer's display settings to a particular theme, such as space or underwater. Desktop Themes also have sound effects. If you want to hear them, make sure your speakers are attached to your computer.

Open Desktop Themes

To open Desktop Themes, open the Start menu, then the Settings submenu. Click on *Control Panel*. The Control Panel contains programs which enable you to change different parts of your computer system. Double-click on the Desktop Themes icon. A dialog box like the one below will open.

The Desktop Themes icon

Save your current scheme

When you first open the Desktop Themes box, the example display shows what your desktop and windows currently look like.

Before changing your display scheme, it is a good idea to save your current display settings in case you want to change back to them later. To do this, click on the *Save As* button. Type in a name for your scheme in the *File name* box, and click on *Save*. Your scheme will be saved onto the *Theme* drop-down list. You can change back to it at any time by selecting its name from this list.

Try out a theme

To try out a theme, select one from the *Theme* drop-down list in the Desktop Themes box. The example display will change to show what your desktop and windows will look like with that theme.

This is the Desktop Themes box.

This is the Desktop Themes box with the Underwater theme selected.

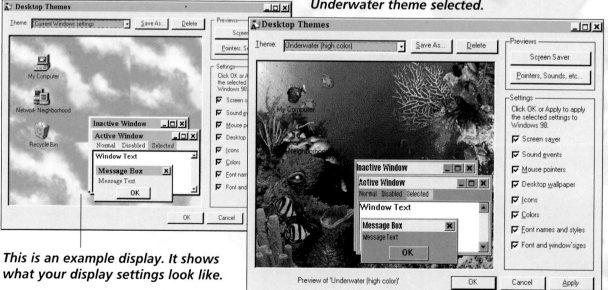

This is an example display. It shows what your display settings look like.

Screen saver preview

As well as your desktop and windows, other parts of your display change when you use a desktop theme. You can see what these will look like using the *Previews* section of the Desktop Themes box. Click on the *Screen Saver* button to try out a screen saver. Move your mouse to close it.

Here are two Desktop Themes screen savers.

Space

Nature

Different pointers

The pointer symbols change to match each theme. To see what your pointers will look like in a selected theme, click on *Pointers, Sounds, etc.* in the *Previews* section. On the Pointers  property sheet of the dialog box that opens, select an option from the *Mouse pointer type* list. The pointer symbol for that option will be displayed in the *Preview* box. Below are some examples of different theme pointer symbols which all show that your computer is busy.

Here are some theme pointer symbols.

Normal settings   **Dangerous Creatures**   **Science**   **Mystery**

Tip: No Desktop Themes?

If you cannot find the Desktop Themes icon in the Control Panel it might be because it has not been put onto your computer yet. To add it, you will need to use the Windows® 98 CD-ROM. See page 77 to find out how to put missing programs onto your computer.

Sound effects

The themes have sound effects which are played when your computer does certain tasks, such as opening or closing a program. Each desktop theme has a different set of sound effects. To hear them, make sure your speakers are switched on.

You can listen to the sound effects of a selected desktop theme using the *Previews* section. Click on *Pointers, Sounds, etc.*, and look at the Sounds property sheet in the dialog box that opens. The *Sound event* list shows different tasks. Any task with a tick beside it has a sound which will be played when the computer does that task. Select a task in this list, then click on the Play button to listen to the sound effect.

Play button

Choose parts of a theme

You can use some parts of a theme and not others. In the *Settings* section of the Desktop Themes box, use the tick boxes to choose which parts of your display you want to be included in the theme you have chosen. Click on *OK* to put the theme into action.

Making things easier

In Windows® 98, there are ways of making your computer easier to use. For example, you can change the way your mouse works, or you can make your display easier to see.

Mouse settings

To change the way your mouse works, you need to use the Mouse Properties box.

Mouse

Open the Start menu, the Settings submenu and then click on *Control Panel*. Double-click on the Mouse icon to open the dialog box.

Double-click speed

You can change how quickly you need to double-click. To do this, use the Buttons property sheet in the Mouse Properties box. In the *Double-click speed* section, there is a slide bar. Drag the marker along the slide bar towards *Slow* or *Fast* to change the double-click speed. To test the speed, double-click in the *Test area*. A jack-in-the-box will pop up if you double-click quickly enough. If not, alter the speed and try again. Your Mouse Properties box may be different from the one described here, depending on the kind of mouse you have.

This is the Double-click speed section of the Mouse Properties box.

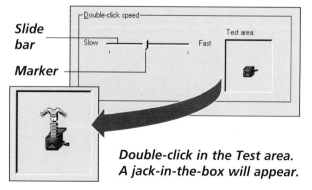

Slide bar

Marker

Double-click in the Test area. A jack-in-the-box will appear.

Accessibility Wizard 98

If you have problems seeing your display, a program called Accessibility Wizard may be able to help you make your computer easier to use. The program offers options such as making the text on the display bigger, or displaying it in contrasting colours, so it is easier to see. To open the Accessibility Wizard, open the Start menu, the Programs submenu, the Accessories submenu, and the Accessibility submenu. Click on *Accessibility Wizard*. A dialog box like the one below will appear. If you can't find the program, see page 77.

This shows the first step of the Accessibility Wizard.

Accessibility Wizard

Welcome to the Accessibility Wizard

This wizard helps you configure Windows for your vision, hearing, and mobility needs.

Click or use the arrow keys to select the smallest text you can read.

Use normal text size for Windows.

Use large window titles and menus.

Use Microsoft Magnifier, and large titles and menus.

< Back   Next >   Cancel

This option is selected.

How to use the Wizard 98

The Accessibility Wizard is a series of dialog boxes. To use it, choose an option from those offered, and then click on *Next* to go to the next set of choices. When there are no more options, a *Finish* button will appear. Click on it to close the Wizard.

In the Accessibility Wizard, there is a button marked *Restore Default Settings*. Click on it if you want to change your display back to the automatic settings.

Sharing your computer

If you share your computer with other people, each person may want to use different display settings, such as Desktop Themes or screen savers. Windows® 98 allows you to save individual settings so that each computer user can use their own settings each time they use the computer.

Set up different users ⑱

Users To tell Windows® 98 that different people use your computer, you need to open a program called User Wizard. To do this, open the Start menu, the Settings submenu, and then the Control Panel. Double-click on the Users icon. The User Wizard, shown below, will open. It works in a similar way to the Accessibility Wizard.

This shows the first step of the User Wizard.

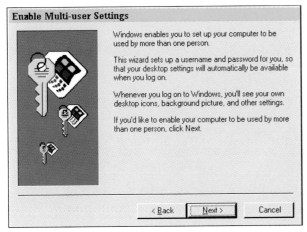

The Wizard displays instructions which tell you what to do to name a user. Read the instructions, and then click on *Next*.

Another box will appear, asking you to type in a name for the first user. Type it into the box provided, and click on *Next*.

Passwords ⑱

The next box asks you to set a password. Each user needs their own password. This means that when you switch on the computer, a password box will appear. You type in your password to use your own settings. When setting a password, make sure you choose one you'll remember easily. Type it into both boxes and click on *Next*.

Personalized Items Settings ⑱

The next step of the Wizard lets you choose the items for which you want to have your own settings. Make your choices using the tick boxes. Beneath the tick boxes, select the option *Creates copies of the current items and their content*. This means you will be able to change the settings on your own files, without changing anyone else's files. Click on *Next*. The next step tells you that you have finished. Click on *Finish* to set up the user.

If you double-click on the Users icon again, a box will appear listing any user names you have set up. To add another user, click on the *New User* button. This will open the User Wizard again.

Swap users

If your computer is on and a different user wants to use it, you don't need to switch the computer off. To change user, open the Start menu and select *Log Off*. The next user can then type in their user name and password to change to their own settings.

Entertainment

You can use your computer to listen to music CDs, mix your own sounds (see page 48) and play video clips. Windows® 98 includes several programs which you can use for these activities. To use them, you need to have speakers and a microphone attached to your computer and switched on.

Multimedia on CD-ROM

You can buy programs, such as encyclopedias, to use on your computer that combine video clips, text, sound and pictures. A program like this is called a multimedia program.

Most multimedia programs you can buy are on CD-ROM. A CD-ROM is a disk which stores information. To use a CD-ROM, insert it into the CD-ROM drive on your computer.

A CD-ROM looks like this.

Play music on your computer

You can listen to music on your computer. To do this, insert a music CD into the CD-ROM drive. The CD Player window will open and the CD will start playing automatically. If you have other programs open, the CD Player window may appear minimized, as a button on your Taskbar. If so, maximize it by clicking on its button.

CD Player

The buttons on the CD Player window look like those on a real CD player. If you point at a button, a ToolTip will appear, telling you what it is for. Click on a button to use it.

This is the CD Player window.

Select a track to play from this drop-down list.

The Options menu enables you to play the tracks on your CD in different ways. Select *Continuous Play* to play the CD over and over again instead of stopping at the end; select *Random Order* to play the tracks in a different order each time.

Type the name of your CD

You can type in the name of the music CD you are playing. Whenever you play that particular CD again, your computer will recognize it and show its name in the CD Player window. To do this, open the Disc menu and select *Edit Play List*. The Disc Settings box will open. Type the details of the CD you are playing into the *Title* and *Artist* sections of the dialog box (see page 47).

Name each track

Using the Disc Settings box, you can type in the name of each track on your music CD. For example, to name the first track, click on *Track 1* in the *Available Tracks* list. *Track 1* will appear in the section at the bottom of the dialog box (see below). Delete *Track 1* from this box, then type in the name of the track. Click on the *Set Name* button to store the name. The track names will appear in the *Track* section of the CD Player window.

This is the Disc Settings box.

Type the artist's name in here.

Type the CD name in here.

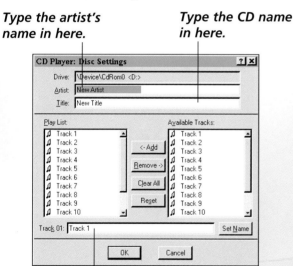

Type the individual track names in here.

Tip: Free videos and sounds

If you are connected to the Internet (see pages 50-53), you can use files that are stored on other computers around the world. This enables you to find lots of free multimedia files, such as video clips and music samples, to use on your computer.

Playing videos 98

You can watch video clips on your computer using a program called ActiveMovie™. There are some video clips you could try out on the Windows® 98 CD-ROM.

To watch one of these video clips, put the Windows® 98 CD-ROM into your CD-ROM drive. A window will appear on your screen. Click on the *Cool Video Clips* option. Another window will open containing lots of video file icons. Double-click on an icon to play a video clip. ActiveMovie™ will open automatically and play the clip in a window on your display.

You can play, pause, or stop a video by clicking on the buttons in the ActiveMovie™ window. The marker on the slide bar at the bottom of the window moves as the video clip is playing. You can drag this marker to rewind or fast-forward the video.

This is a still from a video clip called Mutant from the Windows® 98 CD.

Make some noise

Windows® 98 includes a program called Sound Recorder, which you can use to record, mix and play sounds. This section shows you how to record your own sound effects. You can then set your computer to play these sounds whenever it does certain tasks.

To be able to use Sound Recorder, you need speakers or headphones and a microphone attached to your computer and switched on.

Open Sound Recorder

To open Sound Recorder, open the Start menu, the Programs submenu, the Accessories submenu, and then the Entertainment submenu.

Click on *Sound Recorder* to open the program. The window shown below will open. The buttons on the window are like those on a tape recorder. To use a button, click on it. For example, if you click on the Seek to End button, Sound Recorder will fast forward to the end of an open sound file.

This is the Sound Recorder window.

The green line becomes wavy when a sound is played or recorded.

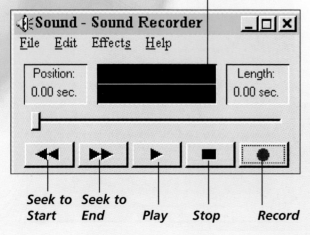

Seek to Start **Seek to End** **Play** **Stop** **Record**

Record a sound

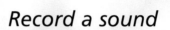

To record sound using Sound Recorder, click on the Record button. Use the microphone to record a sound, such as your voice. To stop recording, click on the Stop button.

To listen to a sound you have recorded, click on the Play button. If you like the recording, you can save it in your My Documents folder. Then, to record another sound, open the File menu and select *New*.

Add effects

Once you have recorded a sound, you can add various effects to it. You can add an echo, speed the sound up, or play it in reverse. These effect options are listed on the Effects menu. If you want to keep a copy of the original recording, make sure you save the recording before changing it.

Try out an effect by clicking on its name. You can click on some effects, such as *Echo*, more than once to make them stronger.

Mix sounds

You can mix different sound files together in Sound Recorder. This means they will play at the same time. To do this, first open a sound file you have saved. In the Sound Recorder window, open the File menu and select *Open*. The Open box will appear. Browse in this box to find the My Documents folder. Select a file and click on *Open*. The file will open in Sound Recorder.

Next, open the Edit menu and select *Mix with File*. Another dialog box will appear. Select another sound file from the My Documents folder and click on *Open*. This file will be mixed with the first. Click on the Play button to hear the mixed sounds.

Combine sounds

You can also insert one sound file into another, so that it interrupts the original file as it is playing. To do this, first open a file in Sound Recorder. Play the file, and click on the Stop button at the point where you want the second file to begin. Then open the Edit menu and select *Insert File.* A dialog box will open for you to choose the second file, as described above.

Set sound effects

You can set your computer to play a sound whenever it does a particular task, such as opening a program. Windows® 98 has some sounds that you can use. You can also use sounds you have recorded yourself as sound effects.

Open Sounds Properties

To set your computer to play sound effects, you need to use the Sounds Properties box. To open it, open the Start menu, the Settings submenu and select *Control Panel*. Click on the Sounds icon, shown here. The dialog box shown below will open.

Sounds

This is the Sounds Properties box.

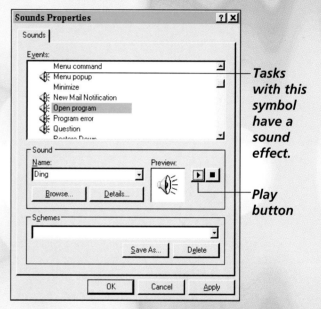

Tasks with this symbol have a sound effect.

Play button

To set a sound to a task, select a task from the *Events* list. You can use one of the Windows® 98 sounds, by selecting one from the *Name* drop-down list. To use one of your own recordings instead, click on the *Browse* button. In the dialog box that opens, find the My Documents folder and double-click on a sound file stored there. The sound will be set to accompany the selected task. To try out the sound, click on the Play button. Click on *OK* in the Sounds Properties box to use the sound effects you have set.

Introducing the Internet

The Internet, called the Net for short, is the name given to a huge network of computers across the world. A network is made up of lots of computers connected together so they can share information. Using Windows® 98, you can connect your computer to the Internet (see page 52), and gain access to a whole world of exciting information. This is called going online. This section gives you an idea of what you can use the Internet for.

E-mail 98

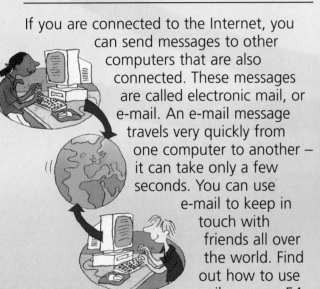

If you are connected to the Internet, you can send messages to other computers that are also connected. These messages are called electronic mail, or e-mail. An e-mail message travels very quickly from one computer to another – it can take only a few seconds. You can use e-mail to keep in touch with friends all over the world. Find out how to use e-mail on page 54.

Newsgroups 98

A newsgroup is a discussion group using e-mail. Newsgroups enable you to get in touch with a group of people who have an interest in the same topic as you and exchange e-mail messages about that topic. You can find newsgroups on the Internet for almost any subject, from pop stars to outer space. Find out how to join and use a newsgroup on page 56.

Online chat 98

Another way of using the Internet to talk to people is to chat online. You use your keyboard to type in a message which can be read immediately by other Internet users. They can then type in replies, which you will see on your display. In this way you can have online conversations with people. On page 58 you can find out how to use an online chat program called Microsoft® Chat, which is included in Windows® 98.

This is what the Microsoft® Chat window looks like with an online conversation in progress.

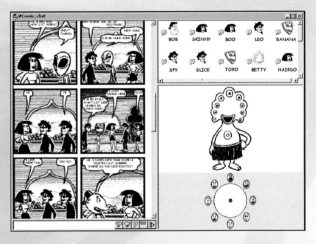

⚠ Warning

You should not give personal details, such as your home address or telephone number, to people you talk to when using the Internet. Remember that someone you communicate with on the Internet is a stranger, so you should treat them in the same way as you would treat anybody you don't know.

The World Wide Web

The World Wide Web, or the Web, is an exciting part of the Internet. It is made up of millions of documents called Web pages. Web pages are created by individual people and by organizations, such as universities and businesses, from around the world.

You can find information about almost anything on the Web, including music, travel, films, games, art and space. Find out how to use the Web on pages 60 to 65.

You can also make your own pages to put onto the Web for other people to look at. Find out how to do this on pages 68 to 71.

Here are some examples of the kinds of information you can find on the Web.

Maps of cities
www.streetmap.co.uk

Weather forecasts
www.boardcast.net

earth.jsc.nasa.gov

Information about space

www.vam.ac.uk

Museums and galleries

Information about film festivals

www.virginradio.com

Radio stations

www.filmfestivals.com/cannes98

www.gamespot.co.uk/pix

Computer games

www.gamespot.co.uk/pix

51

Windows® 98 includes a program called Internet Connection Wizard, which helps you connect to the Internet. This section gives you tips about what you need in order to connect to the Internet, and shows you how to use the Wizard.

How computers are connected

You can use a telephone line to connect your computer to the Internet. In order to send and receive information through a telephone line, your computer may need an extra piece of equipment called a modem. When your computer sends information, the modem changes it into a form that can be sent along telephone lines. When your computer receives information, the modem changes the information back into a form your computer can understand.

Using modems, information can be sent via telephone lines between computers all over the world.

Browsers 98

To be able to look at Web pages, you need to use a type of program called a browser. There are various browser programs available. Windows® 98 includes one called Internet Explorer. Find out how to use it on page 60.

The Internet Explorer icon

Internet service providers

To connect your computer to the Net, you need to use a company called an Internet service provider (ISP). ISPs have computers which are permanently connected to the Net. They let you connect your computer to theirs.

These are the logos of some popular Internet service providers (ISPs).

There are many ISPs to choose from. You can find out details and contact telephone numbers for different ISPs from Internet magazines. Ring up a few companies and compare their prices and services before choosing which one to use. Many of the companies will charge you a fee, but some ISPs are free to use.

Choose an ISP 98

Windows® 98 has a program called Internet Connection Wizard, which can help you set up a connection to the Internet.

The Connect to the Internet icon

To open the Wizard, double-click on the Connect to the Internet icon on your desktop. The first step of the Wizard, shown below, will appear on your display.

The Internet Connection Wizard looks like this.

Internet Connection Wizard

Welcome to the Internet Connection wizard, the easy way to get connected to the Internet. You can use this wizard to set up a new or existing Internet account.

Click the option you want, and then click Next.

- I want to sign up and configure my computer for a new Internet account. (If you select this option make sure your telephone line is connected to your modem.)
- I have an existing Internet account through my phone line or a local area network (LAN). Help me set up my computer to connect to this Internet account.
- My computer is already set up for the Internet. Do not show this wizard again.

Next >   Cancel

The Wizard will take you step by step through the process of selecting an ISP to use. Once you have chosen an ISP, an icon representing that ISP will appear on your desktop. Icons for other programs you need may also appear. Click on *Finish* to close the Wizard. The Connect to the Internet icon will disappear from your desktop.

Open an ISP account 98

Next, you need to set up an account with your ISP. To do this, double-click on the ISP icon on your desktop. A Wizard will open, which will guide you through the process

of opening your ISP account. This process varies, depending on the ISP you have chosen. Follow the instructions the Wizard gives you. You will need to type in a credit card number to pay for connecting to and using the Internet. Ask the owner of the credit card first. All this information will be sent to the ISP via the Internet when you sign in (see below).

Sign in

When you first open a program which uses the Internet, such as Internet Explorer, another program will open automatically. This program will send the details you have typed to your ISP and will connect your computer to theirs. This is called signing in.

To sign in, double-click on the Internet Explorer icon. The sign in program will start. Sign in programs vary depending on the ISP you are using. When you have typed in all the details, click on the *Connect* button. Your computer will connect to the ISP, and is ready for you to use the Internet.

Tip: Getting help

Your Internet service provider should have a helpline telephone number. If you have any problems connecting to, or using the Internet, phone this number to ask for help.

Messages with e-mail ⓽⑧

Once your computer is connected to the Internet, you can use it to send messages, or e-mails, to other computers that are connected. Windows® 98 includes a program called Outlook™ Express, which you can use to send and receive e-mail.

Open Outlook™ Express

The Outlook™ Express icon

To open Outlook™ Express, click on its icon, which you will find on your Quick Launch bar. If the icon is not there, you can open the program by opening the Start menu, the Programs submenu, then the Internet Explorer submenu, and clicking on *Outlook Express*.

The first time you open the program, a dialog box will appear asking you to confirm which folder will be used to store your messages. Click on *OK*. Next, another dialog box may appear, asking if your computer should check for new messages. Click on *OK*. Your computer will connect to the Internet and the Outlook™ Express window, shown below, will open.

This is the Outlook™ Express window.

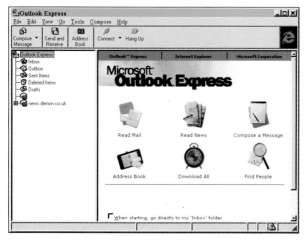

The Outlook™ Express window

The folders listed in the left-hand pane of the Outlook™ Express window will contain e-mail messages that you receive or send. For example, the Inbox will store messages you receive and the Outbox will store messages that are waiting to be sent. Click on a folder in the left-hand pane to show its contents in the right-hand pane.

Write an e-mail message

Each e-mail user has their own e-mail address. Your ISP will tell you what yours is. To send someone an e-mail, like when sending a letter, you need to ask them for their address first.

To write an e-mail, click on the *Compose a Message* button on the Toolbar. A New Message window will open. In the *To* box, type the e-mail address that you want to send the message to. In the *Subject* box, type a short description of what the e-mail is about. Then click on the page area and type in your message.

This is a New Message window.

Type the e-mail address you are writing to here.   **Type the subject of your e-mail here.**

Type your message in the page area.

Send an e-mail message

When you have finished writing your e-mail, click on the *Send* button, shown below, to send it. The e-mail will disappear from your display. If you are online, the e-mail will be sent straight away. If not, it will be stored in the Outbox folder and sent the next time you connect to the Internet (see page 57).

Send button

Read your mail

The Inbox in the left-hand pane of the Outlook™ Express window contains your incoming mail. If *Inbox* is in **bold** type then it contains mail that you haven't read yet. To read your e-mail, click on *Inbox* in the left-hand pane. The right-hand pane will show the contents of the Inbox. The top half of the pane shows a list of the messages you have received. To read a particular message, click on it. It will appear in the bottom half of the pane.

This is the Inbox displaying a message which has been received.

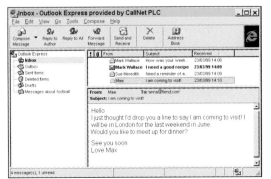

Reply to mail

If you want to reply to a message someone has sent you, click on the message and then click on the *Reply to Author* button, shown below. Another message window, addressed to the person who sent you the message, will open. You can then simply type in your message and click on *Send*.

Reply to Author button

Send a file by e-mail

You can send files by e-mail. For example, you could send a picture file to a friend.

To do this, click on the *Compose a Message* button. In the New Message window that opens, click on the paperclip icon, shown below. An Insert File box will open. Use it to find the file you want to send. Double-click on the file. The box will close and the file will appear as an icon at the bottom of the New Message window. If you receive a file in an e-mail, double-click on the file's icon to open it.

This shows an e-mail message with two files inserted into it.

Paperclip icon

Inserted files

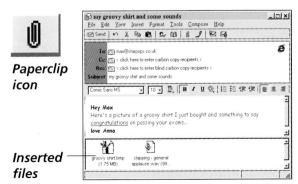

Using newsgroups

You can join a newsgroup to exchange e-mail messages with a group of people about a particular topic that interests you. Newsgroups are free to use; all you pay for is the Internet.

Get a list of newsgroups

To look at a list of newsgroups you need to use the program Outlook™ Express. Open Outlook™ Express, and select *Outlook Express* in the left-hand pane. Then double-click on the *Read News* icon in the right-hand pane. A box will open, asking if you would like to see a list of newsgroups. Click on *Yes*.

Your computer will then prepare a list of newsgroups for you to look at. There are thousands of newsgroups in the list, so this may take a few minutes. When your computer is ready, the Newsgroups window, shown below, will open.

Find an interesting newsgroup

To find a newsgroup that interests you, type the name of a topic, for example *film*, into the *Display newsgroups which contain* box in the Newsgroups window. The *Newsgroups* list will change to show names of newsgroups which contain the letters you type.

Read some messages

To look at a particular newsgroup, select its name, then click on the *Go to* button. The Newsgroups window will close and the right-hand pane of the Outlook™ Express window will split into two sections. The top section lists all the messages that have been sent to that newsgroup. To read a message, click on it. The message will be shown in the lower section of the window. If you want to open the Newsgroups window again, click on the *Newsgroups* button on the Toolbar.

This is the Newsgroups window. It shows a list of all the available newsgroups.

This is the Outlook™ Express window displaying a newsgroup about film festivals.

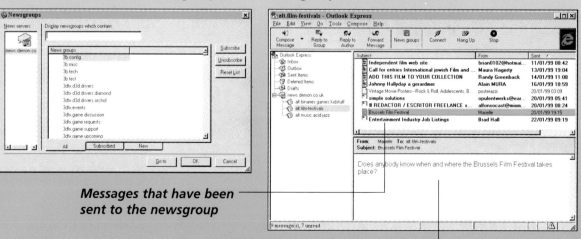

Messages that have been sent to the newsgroup

Any message selected in the top half of the window appears here.

Join a newsgroup

Each newsgroup you look at is listed in the left-hand pane of the Outlook™ Express window. To join a newsgroup right-click on its name in the left-hand pane and select *Subscribe to this newsgroup* from the menu that opens. Its name will turn **bold**.

The Outlook™ Express window lists newsgroups you have joined in the left-hand pane.

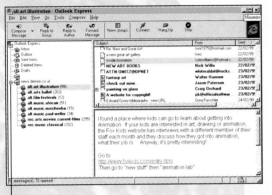

Click on this sign to show or hide the names of newsgroups you have joined.

When you open Outlook™ Express again, any newsgroups you have joined will be listed in the left-hand pane. Click on one to display it in the right-hand pane.

To leave a newsgroup you have joined, right-click on its name in the left-hand pane and select *Unsubscribe from this newsgroup*.

Blue underlined text

In some newsgroup messages you will see pieces of blue underlined text, like this: http://www.nasa.gov
This is a hyperlink (see page 61). It enables you to look at a Web page on the World Wide Web. If you click on it, a window will open to show the Web page.

Write to a newsgroup

To send a message or a question for all members of a newsgroup to see, click on the Compose Message button in the Outlook™ Express window. A New Message window will appear, addressed to the newsgroup. You can then type your message.

If you want to reply to a particular message someone has written, click on the *Reply to Group* button. To send a reply to the person who wrote a particular message, click on the *Reply to Author* button. A Message window will appear addressed directly to that person, instead of to the newsgroup. To send a message you have written, click on the *Send* button.

Connecting and disconnecting

It is a good idea to disconnect from the Internet while writing a long message. This saves money on your Internet connection. To disconnect, click on the *Hang Up* button. When you are ready to send the message, click on the *Connect* button, and your computer will connect to the Internet again.

Use these buttons to connect to and disconnect from the Internet.

Connect   Hang Up

⚠ Warning

When you write to a newsgroup, anyone can use your e-mail address. You might receive rude messages as well as useful replies. To get rid of a message you don't want, right-click on it and select *Delete*.

Chatting online 🌐98

 You can have conversations with people on the Internet using your keyboard to type what you want to say. This is called online chat. Windows® 98 includes a program called Microsoft® Chat which enables you to chat to people online.

Open Microsoft® Chat

Microsoft® Chat looks like a comic strip, in which you and the people you chat to are characters. Everyone who is connected can see the comic strip.

To open Microsoft® Chat, open the Start menu, the Programs submenu, then the Internet Explorer submenu, and click on *Microsoft Chat*. The Chat Connection box, shown below, will open.

Fill in your details

In the Chat Connection box, use the Personal Info property sheet to fill in details about yourself. These details will be available to other people you chat to. Type in your name and a nickname you would like to use when chatting. It is probably best not to type in your e-mail address here, as you might not want everyone you meet to be able to send you e-mails.

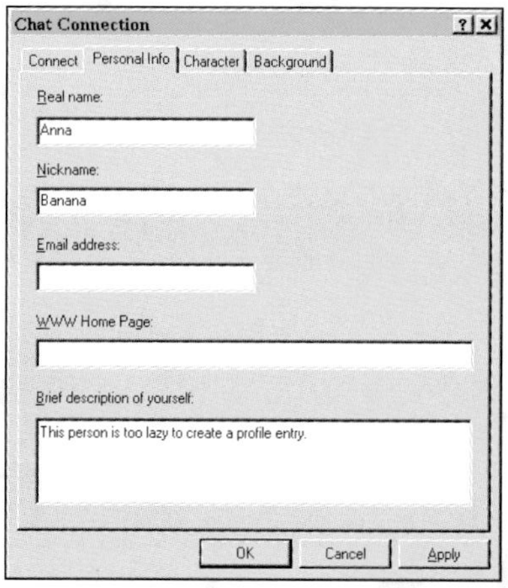

This is the Chat Connection box.

Connect to a chat room

A chat room is a group of people chatting on the same comic strip. There are many chat rooms to choose from. To select one, you need to use the Chat Connection box.

To open a list of chat rooms to choose from, select the option *Show all available chat rooms* on the Connect property sheet of the Chat Connection box, then click on *OK*. The Chat Room List box, shown below, will open.

This is the Chat Room List box.

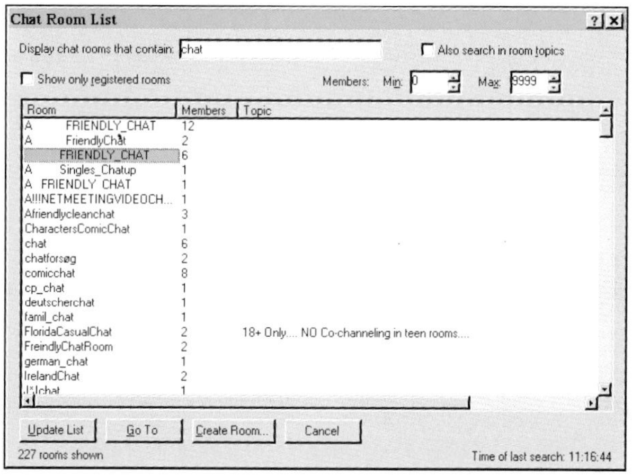

The Chat Room List box lists the chat rooms available. The number in the *Members* column shows how many people are using each chat room. You can find a good chat room by typing a word such as *chat* or *friendly* into the *Display chat rooms that contain* box. The list will change to show chat rooms with that word in their name. Most of the chat rooms are English-speaking but some are in other languages.

Select a chat room that interests you and click on the *Go To* button. Your computer will then connect you to that chat room on the Internet.

Choose a character

You can choose a character to use in the chat room. To do this, open the View menu and select *Options*. The Chat Options box will appear. On the Character property sheet, shown here, click on a name in the *Character* list.

The character will appear in the *Preview* box. When you find one you like, click on *OK* to use it.

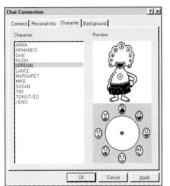

This is the Character property sheet.

Entering and leaving

Enter a chat room by clicking on the Enter Room button on the Toolbar (see picture below). You can leave by clicking on the Leave Room button. If you want to choose a different chat room, open the Room menu and select *Room List* to open the Chat Room List box.

Start chatting

To start chatting, type what you want to say into the bar at the bottom of the Microsoft® Chat window. Click on the speech bubble at the end of the bar to make your text appear in the comic strip. The picture below shows some tips about how to chat.

This shows a typical chat in Microsoft® Chat, and gives some chatting tips.

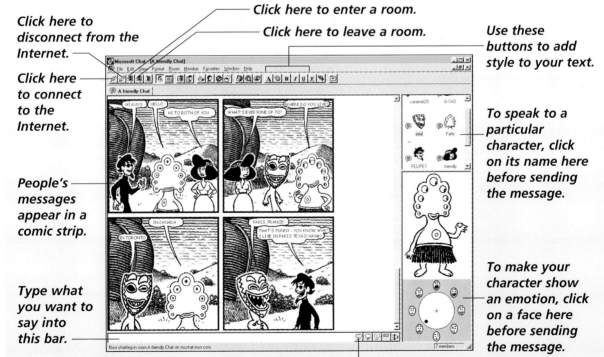

Click here to disconnect from the Internet.

Click here to connect to the Internet.

Click here to enter a room.

Click here to leave a room.

Use these buttons to add style to your text.

People's messages appear in a comic strip.

To speak to a particular character, click on its name here before sending the message.

Type what you want to say into this bar.

To make your character show an emotion, click on a face here before sending the message.

Click on this speech bubble to send the message to the comic strip.

The World Wide Web is made up of millions of Web pages. A collection of Web pages grouped together is called a Web site. You can find Web sites about every subject imaginable. To be able to look at Web pages, you need a program called a browser. Windows® 98 includes a browser called Internet Explorer.

Open Internet Explorer

To open Internet Explorer, click on its icon on your Quick Launch bar. When you open

Internet Explorer

your browser it will automatically show you a particular Web page. This is called the default page. It varies, depending on who your ISP is.

Web addresses

Every Web page has its own address so you can find it on the Web. A Web address is also called a URL (Uniform Resource Locator).

The address of the page you are looking at appears in the Address bar at the top of the window. You can open a Web page by typing its address into the Address bar and pressing the Return key on your keyboard.

Try typing this address into the Address bar: *www.nationalgeographic.com* (don't leave any spaces between the characters). A Web page similar to the one shown below will appear in your browser window. The page may take a little while to appear. You have to wait for it to be found and transferred onto your computer. This is called downloading a Web page.

This is the Internet Explorer window showing a Web page.

The Address bar

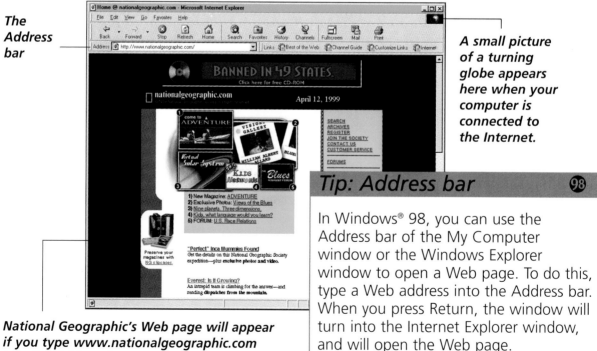

A small picture of a turning globe appears here when your computer is connected to the Internet.

National Geographic's Web page will appear if you type www.nationalgeographic.com into the Address bar.

Tip: Address bar ❸⓼

In Windows® 98, you can use the Address bar of the My Computer window or the Windows Explorer window to open a Web page. To do this, type a Web address into the Address bar. When you press Return, the window will turn into the Internet Explorer window, and will open the Web page.

Browsing using hyperlinks

There is another easy way of looking at different Web pages, or browsing on the Web, without having to know the Web address of each page you look at. Pages on the Web are linked to other pages by hyperlinks. Hyperlinks are words and pictures on a Web page that work as entrance points to other Web pages. To use a hyperlink, simply click on it.

You can tell if something on a Web page is a hyperlink because when you move your pointer over it, the symbol will turn into a hand, shown below.

The main picture shows Web pages found by clicking on hyperlinks.

This shows how you can jump between Web pages by clicking on hyperlinks.

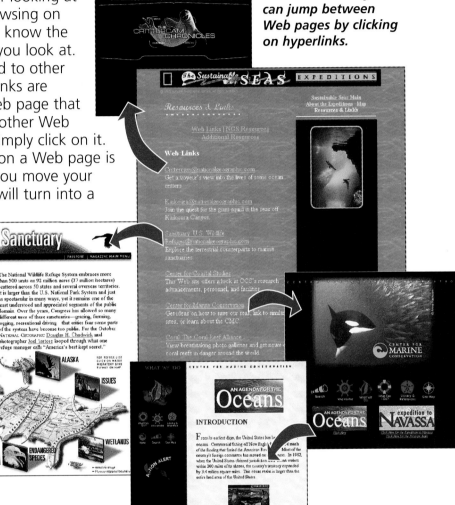

A hand pointer symbol

Browsing tools

The Internet Explorer window has browsing tools like those in the My Computer window. When you are browsing the Web, you can use the *Back* and *Forward* buttons on the Toolbar to retrace your steps and look at Web pages you have looked at before.

Stop

If your computer takes too long to download a particular Web page, or it has started to download a page that you decide you don't want to look at after all, you can stop it. To do this, click on the *Stop* button, shown here.

Anyone can make Web pages about any subject and put them anywhere on the Web. There are programs you can use which make it easy to find information on the Web. This section shows you how to search for interesting and fun information.

Search services

If you are looking for information about a particular topic, whether that topic is pop trivia or scientific research, you can search the Web for pages about that subject.

To search the Web you can use a type of program called a search engine to help you. There are lots of different search engines you can use. They are stored on the Web.

To use a search engine, click on the *Search* button on the Internet Explorer Toolbar. A pane will appear in the left-hand side of the window, showing a list of search engines you can use.

This shows how to use a search engine.

This button opens a list of search engines.

Search the Web

To start a search, select a search engine from the list. In the text box, type a word or words that describe the topic you are looking for as closely as possible. It is important to use a name or a phrase that is key to the topic. For example, if you want information about space, you could type the word *space* into the box. If you want to know about the Hubble Space Telescope, then you could type the word *hubble* into the box. Click on the *Search* button next to the text box to begin the search.

Search results

The results of the search will be listed in the left-hand pane of the window. This list consists of hyperlinks to pages that were found. Click on a hyperlink to display that Web page in the right-hand pane.

The picture below shows some Web sites that were found using the MSN search engine, searching with the word *hubble*.

Click on hyperlinks in the left-hand pane to display pages in the right-hand pane.

These are two of the Web pages that were found.

Type a word into the Search text box and click on the Search button next to it.

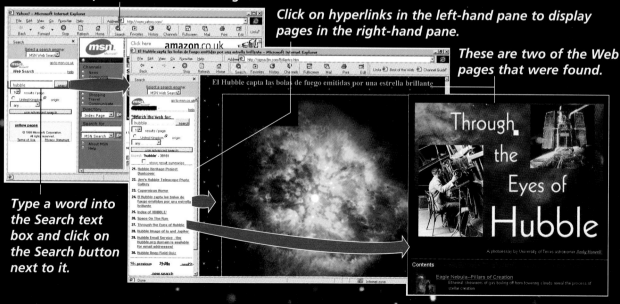

Tip: Good search engines

You can get to a search engine Web page by typing the address of a particular search engine into the Address bar. Here are the addresses of some popular search engines:
http://www.altavista.com
http://www.yahoo.com
http://www.supersnooper.com

Saving and using files

On the Web there are lots of files you will find which you can either open or save onto your computer for free. For example, try searching for *sounds* or *videos* using a search engine. Sound and video files usually appear on Web pages as an underlined text hyperlink. To open or save the file, click on the hyperlink. The File Download box, shown below, will appear. If you just want to play the file, click on *Open this file from its current location*. To save the file onto your computer, select *Save this file to disk* and then click on *OK*. The Save As box will open. Use it to save the file into your My Documents folder.

This is the File Download box.

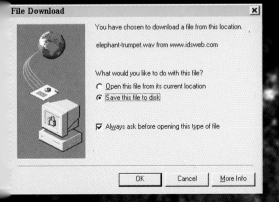

Saving pictures

It's easy to save pictures you find on the Web to use on your computer. You can save them onto your hard disk, or use them as wallpaper on your desktop. To save a picture from the Web, right-click on it and select *Save As* from the context menu. A dialog box will open which you can use to save the picture onto your computer. To use the picture as wallpaper, right-click on it and select *Set Wallpaper* from the context menu.

This picture was set as tiled wallpaper.

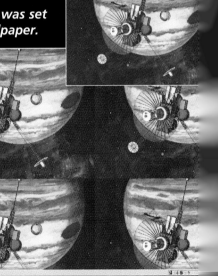

⚠ Warning

People can put any information they like on the Internet. As well as interesting information, you may come across inaccurate, unpleasant or even offensive material. Be careful to avoid anything you don't want to look at.

There are programs called filters which can prevent your browser from opening Web pages containing unsuitable material.

Favourite Web sites

When you find a Web site you like, there is a way of making sure you can find it again easily. Internet Explorer enables you to keep a record of your favourite Web sites, so that you can look at them again and again.

Internet Explorer also provides easy access to some Web sites belonging to large organizations. These are called channels.

Add to your favourites

When you find a Web page that you would like to look at again, open the Favorites menu in the Internet Explorer window and select *Add to Favorites*. The Add Favorite box, shown below, will open.

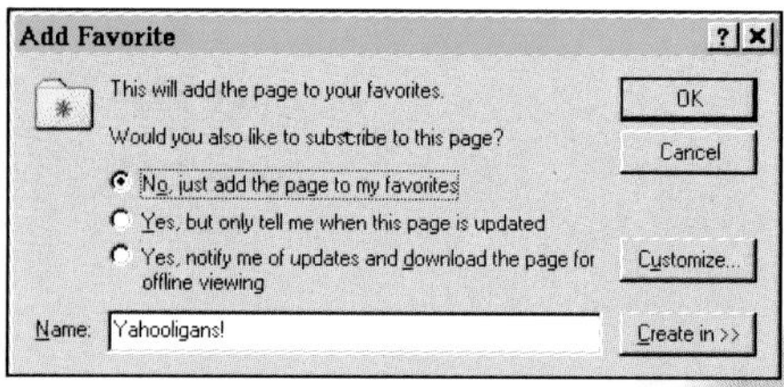

This is the Add Favorite box.

Select *No, just add the page to my favorites* and click on *OK*. This will add the Web page to the list of options on the Favorites menu. To open that page in future, all you need to do is click on its name on the Favorites menu.

Tip: On the Start menu

Any Web page you add to the Favorites menu is automatically listed on the Favorites submenu on the Start menu. You can open the Web page by clicking on its name on this menu. Internet Explorer will open and show the page.

Look at favourite Web pages

If you click on the *Favorites* button in the Internet Explorer window, a pane will appear in the left-hand side of the window, listing the Web pages you have saved as Favorites. Click on a Web page in the Favorites pane to display it in the right-hand pane. You can close the Favorites pane again by clicking on its Close button.

This shows the Internet Explorer window with the Favorites pane open.

Favorites pane Close button

Organize your Favorites menu

If you put a lot of Web pages on the Favorites menu it is a good idea to organize them into folders to make them easier to find. To do this, open the Favorites menu and select *Organize Favorites*. A dialog box like the one shown below will open. Use the buttons in the *Organize* section of the dialog box to create a new folder, and then to move your Favorites into it. You can also rename or delete your Favorites using this dialog box.

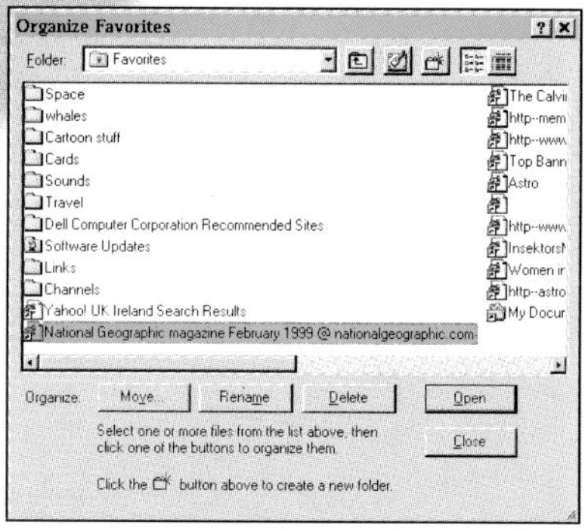

This is the Organize Favorites box.

Open the Channels pane

Internet Explorer gives easy access to certain Web sites called channels. To look at your channels, open the Internet Explorer window and click on the *Channels* button. A pane will appear in the left-hand side of the window listing the available channels.

The Channels button

Tip: Different channels

The channels listed in the Channels pane depend on which country you live in. If you don't have the same channels as the ones shown here you can reach these Web sites by typing their Web addresses (shown on page 80) into the Internet Explorer Address bar.

This is the Internet Explorer window showing the New Scientist channel.

The Channels pane

The BBC Online channel

The RAICAST channel

Open a channel

Click on a channel in the left-hand pane to display it in the right-hand pane of the window. When you first open a particular channel you will see an introductory page. Before you can look at the rest of the site, you have to click on the *Add Active Channel* button. A dialog box will open. Select *No, just keep it in my Channel Bar* and click on *OK*. You will then be able to look at the rest of the Web pages which are included in that channel.

Here are some examples of channels you can look at using Internet Explorer.

The Vogue channel

The Virgin Net channel

Web Style ⑱

Windows® 98 offers ways in which you can make working with the display on your computer more like using the Web. You can use a feature called Web Style to change the way you browse on your computer. Another feature called Active Desktop enables you to put Web pages directly onto your desktop.

Classic or Web Style

In Windows® 98 there are two ways of using your mouse to work with your display. The way described so far is called Classic Style. This is the automatic setting in Windows® 98. However, if you choose a setting called Web Style, instead of double-clicking on an item to open it, you only have to click on it once. Instead of clicking on an item to select it, you only have to point at it.

Open the Folder Options box

To change your display to use Web Style you need to use the Folder Options box. To open it, open the Start menu, the Settings submenu and click on *Folder Options*. The dialog box shown below will open. Click on *Web style* and then click on *OK*. The first time you select Web Style, another dialog box will appear. Select *Yes*, then click on *OK* and your settings will change.

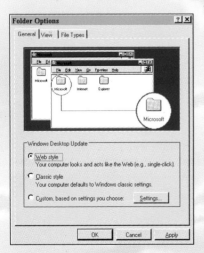

This is the Folder Options box.

Files, folders and programs

Using Web Style, file, folder and program names are underlined so they look like hyperlinks on the Web. They turn blue when you point at them. Also, when you open a folder in My Computer, details of selected files or folders are shown in the left-hand side of the view area. The picture below shows what this looks like.

This shows what the My Documents folder looks like using Web Style.

Details about the selected item are shown in this area.

File, folder and program names are underlined.

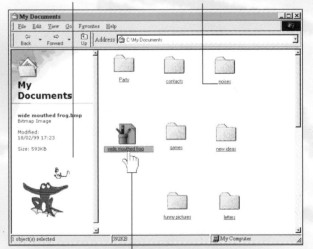

When you point at a file, folder or program, the pointer symbol turns into a hand.

Tip: Customized settings

In the Folder Options box the *Custom* option enables you to combine parts of Web Style and Classic Style. Once you have selected this option, click on the *Settings* button to choose how you want different parts of your display to work.

Activate the Active Desktop

Before you can put Web pages directly onto your desktop, you need to switch Active Desktop on. Right-click on the desktop and select *Properties* from the context menu. The Display Properties box will open. On the Web property sheet, select *View my Active Desktop as a web page*. You can then add the items described here to your desktop.

Add a Channel bar

A Channel bar looks like the Channels pane of the Internet Explorer window, and enables you to open channels directly from your desktop. To put the bar onto your desktop, select *Internet Explorer Channel Bar* on the Web property sheet of the Display Properties box, and click on *Apply*. The Channel bar will appear. To open a channel, just click on its name on the bar. Internet Explorer will open to show the channel.

This is the Channel bar.

Active Desktop Gallery

To visit a Web site which has items to put onto your desktop, click on the *New* button on the Web property sheet of the Display Properties box. A dialog box will open, asking if you want to look at the Microsoft Active Desktop Gallery. Click on *Yes*, and Internet Explorer will open the Web site. Browse to find items you like, and click on the orange *Add to Active desktop* button next to any item to select it.

Subscriptions

When you select an item to put onto your desktop, a dialog box may appear, asking if you are sure. Click on *Yes*. Another dialog box will appear, saying you have chosen to subscribe to the site. Subscribing is free, but it means your computer will automatically connect to the Internet at certain times to update the information contained by the desktop item. Click on *OK* and the item will appear on your desktop. To check or alter how often your computer will connect to the Web to update the item, click on *Customize Subscription* and use the Wizard that opens.

Add a page from the Web

To add a Web page to your desktop, click on the *New* button on the Web property sheet of the Display Properties box, then click on *No* in the dialog box that opens. Another dialog box will open. Type the Web address of the Web page you want to use into the text box provided, and click on *OK* to add it to your desktop.

This is an example of what an Active Desktop can look like with various items on it.

 You can create your own Web page to put onto the World Wide Web using a program included in Windows® 98 called FrontPage Express. This page shows you how to make a basic Web page.

Open FrontPage Express

To open FrontPage Express, open the Start menu, the Programs submenu, then the Internet Explorer submenu and click on *FrontPage Express*. A window will open with a new Web page document in it.

Write some text

Type some text onto your Web page. The Toolbar contains some style buttons like those in WordPad. You can use them to change the colour, style and font of the text. To make text bigger, select the text, then click on the button with the large *A* on it; to make text smaller, click on the button with the small *A*.

Use these buttons to change the text size.

This is the FrontPage Express window with some text typed into it.

Tool bar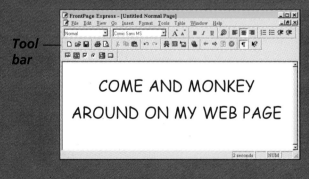

Create a Web page folder

If you want to put pictures and sounds (see page 70) onto your Web page you need to keep them all together in one folder. Use Windows Explorer to create a subfolder in your My Documents folder. Call the subfolder My Web Page.

Picture files on the Web

You can add pictures to your Web page, such as a picture you have created in Paint.

Any picture included on a Web page has to be saved in a particular form. To use a picture you have created in Paint on your Web page you need to save it again. To do this, open the file. In the Paint window, open the File menu and select *Save As*. In the *Save as type* section of the Save As box, select *JPEG (*.JPG, *.jpeg)* from the drop-down list. Choose your My Web Page folder as the location in which to save the picture.

When you save a Paint file as a JPEG file its icon changes. **Paint file icon** **JPEG file icon**

Add a picture

To add a picture to your Web page in FrontPage Express, position your cursor where you want the image to appear. Then click on the Insert Image button, shown here. The Image box will open. Click on the *Browse* button in it and find the JPEG file you saved in the My Web Page folder. Double-click on the file name. The picture will appear on your page.

Insert Image button

Resize the picture

If you click on the image, a frame appears around it. You can make the picture bigger or smaller on your page by dragging the bottom, right-hand corner of the frame.

This shows a Web page with a picture file.

COME AND MONKEY AROUND ON
MY WEB PAGE

A BIT ABOUT MONKEYS

Monkeys and apes belong to a group of animals called primates. There are about 120 species of monkey (like squirrel monkeys and spider monkeys) and 4 species of apes (chimpanzees, gibbons, orang-utans and gorillas). The main difference between monkeys and apes is that monkeys have tails and apes don't. Tails help monkeys to balance as they swing about in the treetops.

To make an image bigger or smaller, drag the picture frame using this corner.

Add a background colour

You can add a background colour to your page. To do this, right-click on the page and select *Page Properties* from the context menu. On the Background property sheet, select a colour from the *Background* drop-down list. If you select *Custom* on the list, the Edit Colors box will open. This offers more colours to choose from. When you have selected a colour, click on *OK* to add it to your page.

Add hyperlinks

You can add hyperlinks to link your page to others on the Web. To do this, type in the address of a Web page and press the Return key. The address will change into a hyperlink, turning blue and underlined. When your page is on the Web, people will be able to click on these hyperlinks to open Web pages.

This shows a Web page with hyperlinks on it.

FrontPage Express - [C:\My Documents\Anna's Web page\annaswe...
File Edit View Go Insert Format Tools Table Window Help

Normal   Comic Sans MS

Some great monkey links:

www.monkeymaddness.com This has lots of monkey pictures and info. Read 'My Life with Chimpanzees' by Jane Goodall (in Articles and Ads).

www.jrcnet.com/duMond This is a monkey reserve - you can adopt a monkey that lives there!

http://home.ici.net/~kend/monkey/monkeydance.html This is a very funny page with lots of dancing monkeys on it.

10 seconds   NUM

Hyperlink   **Add some information about the Web pages your hyperlinks lead to.**

Saving and opening your page

To save your Web page, open the FrontPage Express File menu and select *Save As*. In the Save As box, click on the *As File* button and save the file into your My Web Page folder.

To work on your file again, open FrontPage Express, then select *Open* from the File menu. Select *From File* in the dialog box, and click on *Browse*. Find your file and double-click on it to open it. If you want to see your page as it will look on the Web (you won't be able to work on it), open your My Web page folder and double-click on your Web page's file icon. It will open in Internet Explorer.

More on your Web page **98**

Once you have created a basic Web page there are lots of things you can add using FrontPage Express to make it more fun. You can then put your finished page onto the World Wide Web.

Add a sound

You can add a sound to your Web page which will play when someone opens your page on the Web. To do this, first use Windows Explorer to copy a sound file you have made into the My Web Page folder (see page 31).

Next, open FrontPage Express and open your Web page using the File menu. Open the Insert menu and select *Background Sound*. In the Background Sound box that opens, select *From File* and then click on the *Browse* button. Find the sound file you moved to the My Web Page folder and double-click on it to add it to your Web page. You won't be able to hear the sound in FrontPage Express. To hear it, open your page from your My Web page folder as you did on page 69.

Add moving text

You can add a banner with moving text on it, called a scrolling marquee, to your Web page. To do this, position your cursor where you want the marquee to appear, then open the Insert menu and select *Marquee*. In the dialog box that opens, type some text into the *Text* box, and then select a

Add lines between sections

When you are making a Web page you can make it easy to read by putting horizontal lines between sections to separate them. To do this, position the cursor where you want the line to appear. Open the Insert menu and click on *Horizontal Line*. A line will appear on your page.

E-mail

If you want people to be able to send you e-mails, you can add your e-mail address to your Web page. Type your e-mail address and press the Return key. Your address will turn into a hyperlink. When someone clicks on this hyperlink, their e-mail program will automatically open a New Message window addressed to you, and they can send you a message.

Think carefully before putting your e-mail address on your page. There is a risk that people might send unpleasant messages.

colour for your banner in the *Background Color* box. Click on *OK* to add the marquee to your Web page. When the marquee appears on your page, it won't be moving. To see your page as it will actually look on the Web, you need to open it from your My Web Page folder (see page 69).

This is how a scrolling marquee will look in FrontPage Express.

What do you call a big ape that likes desserts? A m

Tip: Download time

When you open a page on the Web, the time it takes to appear on your display, called downloading, depends on how much information is on it.

When you make a Web page in FrontPage Express, the Status bar at the bottom of the window tells you how long your page should take to download. Try to keep this time as short as possible. You can do this by not adding too many large files, such as sound files or big pictures, to your page.

Keep your files together

If you use a file on your Web page that you haven't saved into your My Web Page folder, when you save your page, a dialog box like the one shown below will appear. It asks whether you would like a copy of the file you have used to be moved to the same folder as your Web page is stored in. Check the name of the folder is My Web Page. If it is not, click on the Browse button and select the My Web Page folder. Then click on the *Yes* button. A copy of the file will be saved into the folder.

If you forget to move a file you are using on your page into your My Web Page folder, this dialog box will appear when you save your Web page.

Save Data to File	✕

Save this file to the local disk?

Save as:

C:\My Documents\My Web Page\seagulls.wav   Browse...

| Yes | Yes to All | No | Cancel | Help |

Put your page on the Web

To put your page onto the Web so people can look at it, you need to store it on a computer which is permanently connected to the Internet. This is called uploading your Web page. Telephone or e-mail your ISP for information about how to do this.

Windows® 98 has a Wizard which can help you to upload your page, once you have the necessary details from your ISP. To open the Wizard, open your page in FrontPage Express, then open the Save As box and click on *OK*. Click on *Yes* in the dialog box that appears. Follow the instructions the Wizard gives you to upload your page onto the Web.

This shows a finished Web page that was made in FrontPage Express.

Scrolling marquee   *Picture*

A hyperlink   *Horizontal line*   *Background colour*

Looking after your computer

 Windows® 98 includes a group of programs called System Tools, which you can use to keep your computer working properly. To open any of the System Tools described here, open the Start menu, the Programs submenu, the Accessories submenu, then the System Tools submenu and click on the name of the program.

ScanDisk

ScanDisk is a program which enables your computer to check its hard disk for faults and mend them. When you open ScanDisk, the dialog box shown below will appear.

This is the ScanDisk box.

![ScanDisk dialog box screenshot showing ScanDisk - (C:), drive selection with 3½ Floppy (A:) and (C:), Type of test with Standard (checks files and folders for errors) selected and Thorough (performs Standard test and scans disk surface for errors) with Options button, Automatically fix errors checked, and Start, Close, Advanced buttons]

In the *Type of test* section of the ScanDisk box, select *Standard*. Make sure the *Automatically fix errors* option is selected - this means that if your computer does find any faults on the disk it will mend them by itself. Click on *Start*, and your computer will begin checking its hard disk for faults. When ScanDisk has finished, another dialog box will appear showing the results of the test. Close the dialog box and click on the *Close* button to close the ScanDisk box.

Tip: Close programs

Before using any of the System Tools, close any other programs which are open. Having other programs open at the same time could prevent the System Tools from being able to do their job.

Disk Defragmenter

When your computer stores files, it puts the pieces of information wherever there is space on the hard disk. Disk Defragmenter is a program which collects the pieces of each file and stores them together on the hard disk. This enables your computer to open files more quickly. It is called defragmenting.

When you open Disk Defragmenter, a dialog box will appear, asking which disk you want to defragment. Check that your computer's hard disk is selected and click on *OK* to start defragmenting. When it has finished, click on *Yes* to close the program.

Disk Cleanup 98

Disk Cleanup is a program which deletes unwanted files to make more space on the hard disk. Don't worry, it won't delete any of the files you have made, unless you have put them in the Recycle Bin. It empties the Recycle Bin and deletes other files you won't miss. When you open the program, a dialog box appears asking which disk you want to clean up. Check your computer's hard disk is selected and click on *OK*. Click on *OK* in the Disk Cleanup box to start cleaning up your hard disk. When Disk Cleanup has finished, its dialog box will close by itself.

Regular maintenance 98

It is a good idea to use the System Tools at least once a month, to keep your computer in good shape. Windows® 98 includes a program called Maintenance Wizard, which you can use to schedule these programs to open automatically at certain times, when you won't be using your computer.

To open the Wizard, open the Start menu, the Programs submenu, the Accessories submenu, then the System Tools submenu, and click on *Maintenance Wizard*. The first part of the Wizard is shown below.

This shows the first part of the Maintenance Wizard.

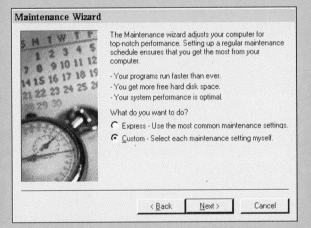

In the first part of the Wizard, select *Custom* and click on *Next*. The Wizard will ask you to choose a time when you can leave your computer on but you won't be using it. Select a time, and click on *Next*. The next box tells you which programs open automatically when Windows® 98 starts. Click on *Next*. The Speed Up Programs box will open. This allows you to set a time for your computer to open Disk Defragmenter. To set a time, click on *Reschedule*. The Reschedule box will open.

The Reschedule box, shown below, enables you to set a time for the Disk Defragmenter to open. Use the options in the box to set a time and then click on *OK* to return to the Wizard.

This is the Reschedule box.

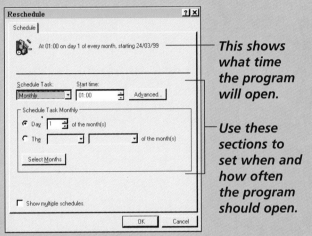

This shows what time the program will open.

Use these sections to set when and how often the program should open.

The next part of the Wizard enables you to set a time for ScanDisk and then for Disk Cleanup. The Wizard will then show you the timetable. Click on *Finish* to close the Wizard.

Change your schedule 98

To change the times the System Tools are set to open, open the Wizard, as before. A dialog box will appear. Select *Change my maintenance settings or schedule* and then use the Wizard to reset the times.

Tip: Stay switched on 98

Remember to leave your computer on at times when the System Tools programs are scheduled to be used, otherwise they won't be able to open.

Help

Windows® 98 has a program called Help which you can use to find out or remind yourself about how parts of Windows® 98 work. Windows® 98 also has a Welcome to Windows tour which you can use to learn more about Windows® 98.

Open Help

To use the Help program, open the Start menu and click on *Help*. The Help window, shown below, will open. It has three property sheets: Contents, Index and Search. These offer different ways of looking for topics you need help with.

This is the Help window showing the Contents property sheet.

The three Property sheets enable you to look for Help in different ways.

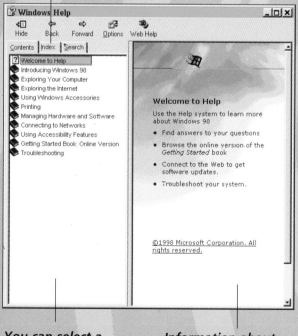

You can select a topic to find out about from this list.

Information about any topic you select will appear here.

Contents

On the Contents property sheet, click on a topic with a book icon next to it and a list of topics about that subject will appear beneath it. If you click on a topic with a question mark icon next to it, information about that topic will appear in the right-hand pane.

Index

The Index property sheet lists topics in alphabetical order. Type a word into the text box and the list will jump to the words in the index which begin with the letters you typed. Select a topic from the index, then click on *Display* to show it in the right-hand pane. If a word in the list has more than one matching topic, a Topics Found box will appear, containing all of the matching topics. Click on one, and then click on *Display* to show it in the right-hand pane.

This shows the Topics Found box listing topics related to the World Wide Web.

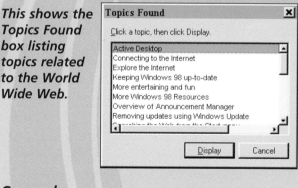

Search

The Search property sheet lets you search for key words in a Help topic. Type a word into the *Type in the keyword to find* box and click on *List Topics*. Topics which contain the word you typed will be listed in the *Topic* box. Select a topic and click on *Display* to show it in the right-hand pane of the Help window.

Underlined words

You can click on an underlined word in the right-hand pane of the Help window to get more information. Sometimes this will display an information box, explaining what the word means. You can close the box by clicking outside it. Some underlined words have a special function. For example, if you click on *Related Topics*, similar topics to the one displayed will be shown in the right-hand pane. If you click on *click here*, you can open a program.

Help in programs

If you are using a program and you need help with it, you can open the Help window from that program. To do this, open the Help menu in the program window and click on *Help Topics*. The Help window will appear, displaying topics relevant to the program you are using.

What's This?

You can get help using dialog boxes. Many dialog boxes have a question mark button next to the Close button. This is called *What's This?* Click on the question mark, then click on a part of the dialog box you want to find out about. An information box will appear giving an explanation of the part you clicked on.

? **The What's This? button**

 When you click on the What's This? button, your pointer symbol changes to look like this.

Welcome to Windows® 98 🕘

When you first start Windows® 98, a Welcome to Windows® 98 box appears on your display. You can use it to take a tour of Windows® 98, to get to know how it works. If the box is not on your display, you can open it using the Start menu. Open the Start menu, the Programs submenu, the Accessories submenu, the System Tools submenu, and click on *Welcome To Windows*. The dialog box shown below will open.

This is the Welcome to Windows® 98 box.

![Welcome to Windows 98 dialog box. Microsoft Windows98. CONTENTS: Register Now, Connect to the Internet ✔, Discover Windows 98, Maintain Your Computer ✔. Welcome — Welcome to the exciting new world of Windows 98, where your computer desktop meets the Internet! Sit back and relax as you take a brief tour of the options available on this screen. If you want to explore an option, just click it. ☑ Show this screen each time Windows 98 starts. Continue]

Take the Windows® 98 tour 🕘

To use the Windows® 98 tour, click on *Discover Windows 98* in the Contents section of the Welcome to Windows® 98 box. Your display will change to show the first stage of the tour. Follow the instructions to find out about Windows® 98. There are different levels, for beginners and more experienced computer users. Each level has its own instructions. Switch on your speakers if you want to hear a voice which guides you through the tour. To close the tour, click on the Close button.

Installing Windows® 98 ⑱

If your computer doesn't have Windows® 98, you need to put it onto your computer. This is called installing. If you already have Windows® 98 on your computer, but you can't find some of the programs described in this book, it may be because they have not been installed. You can install them separately using the Windows® 98 CD-ROM.

What you need

For Windows® 98 to work, you have to have a certain type of computer. You will find instructions on the Windows® 98 packaging which tell you what kind of computer you need to be able to use Windows® 98. This tells you the least powerful kind of computer you need. The more powerful your computer is, the faster and more smoothly Windows® 98 will work.

Upgrading from Windows® 95

Replacing a previous Windows® operating system with Windows® 98 is called upgrading. When you upgrade your operating system, all of the files and folders you created yourself will stay as they are.

If you have Windows® 95 on your computer, Windows® 98 should be easy to install. To do this, switch your computer on, and put the Windows® 98 CD-ROM into the CD-ROM drive of your computer. A dialog box will appear asking whether you want to upgrade. Click on *Yes*, and your computer will start to install Windows® 98.

Upgrading from Windows® 3.1

To upgrade to Windows® 98 from Windows® 3.1, first you need to put the Windows® 98 CD-ROM into your computer's CD-ROM drive. Then open the File Manager program, select the CD-ROM drive and double-click on *Setup.exe*. Your computer will start to install Windows® 98.

Windows® 98 Setup

When the Windows® 98 CD-ROM starts, you will see the Windows® 98 Setup display, shown below. The box in the middle gives instructions about what to do to start installing Windows® 98, and explains each stage of the process.

This is the Windows® 98 Setup display.

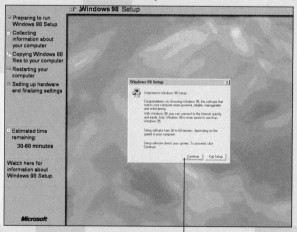

Follow the instructions shown here to install Windows® 98.

Click on *Continue* and the Setup program will check your computer to see what programs are on it and how it is organized. When it has finished, click on *Continue*. A program called the Windows® 98 Setup Wizard will open.

Setup Wizard

The Setup Wizard will guide you through the rest of the installation process. To use the Wizard, follow the instructions it gives, then click on the *Next* button to go on to the next stage of the process. During the installation your computer may need to restart. This means it will automatically shut down and start up again. Below are some tips about the installation process to help you. When the Welcome to Windows® 98 box (see page 75) appears on your display, Windows® 98 is installed and ready to use.

Product Key The Setup Wizard will ask you to type in your Product Key. The Product Key is a code made up of five groups of letters and numbers. You will find it on a label on the Windows® 98 CD-ROM packaging.

Backing up The Wizard will ask whether you want to save your existing files. If you think you may want to take Windows® 98 off your computer again and go back to using the version of Windows you had before, then you should click on *Yes*. Otherwise click on *No*. Saving copies of your files takes up a lot of space on your computer's hard disk, so only do it if your computer has lots of room on its hard disk.

Startup disk The Wizard will ask you to insert a floppy disk into your computer to make a Startup disk. It will copy files onto the disk that your computer uses when Windows® 98 starts up. This disk can be useful if your computer has problems starting up in the future. Label it *Startup* and keep it in a safe place.

Missing programs

If you have Windows® 98 on your computer but certain programs are missing, they might not have been installed with the rest of Windows® 98. You can install single programs from the CD-ROM. Insert the Windows® 98 CD-ROM into your computer's CD-ROM drive. In the window that opens, click on *Add/Remove Software*. The Add/Remove Programs Properties box will open. In the *Components* list on the Windows Setup property sheet, the programs with a tick beside them are already on your computer. Click on any program in the list that you want to install and a tick should appear beside it. Click on *OK* and a dialog box will appear asking whether you want to restart your computer. Click on *Yes*. Your computer will shut down and start up again. When it starts up, the programs you selected will be installed.

Windows Update

Computer programs are continually being updated. Windows® 98 contains a feature called Windows Update which enables you to get the most recent version of Windows® 98 free from the Microsoft Web site. You need to be connected to the Internet to use Windows Update. To use it, open the Start menu and select *Windows Update*. The Internet Explorer window will open showing the Microsoft Windows Update Web site. You can save any updated programs or features onto your computer by following the instructions on the Web site. Saving certain programs may take several hours.

Glossary

Here are explanations of some computer words that you may come across. Any word in *italics* is explained elsewhere in the glossary.

address A description of where to find a piece of information on your computer or on the *Web*.

browser A *program* you can use to find and look at information stored on your computer or on the *Web*.

chat A typed conversation between people, using the *Internet*.

crash A sudden computer breakdown.

download To copy *programs* or *files*, such as Web pages or pictures, that you find on the Internet onto your computer.

e-mail (**electronic mail**) Messages people can send to each other using computers which are connected via the *Internet*.

file Any piece of work, such as a letter or a picture, created using a *program*.

hardware The pieces of equipment which make up a computer, such as the screen, the mouse and the keyboard.

home page 1. An introductory *Web page* which contains links to other pages on a *Web site*; 2. The first *Web page* your *browser* shows when you connect to the *Web* (also called a default page).

hyperlink (**link**) A picture or text on a *Web page* which, when clicked on, tells the *browser* to show another *Web page*.

icon A small picture on your computer display which represents a piece of information or a *program* stored on your computer.

Internet (**Net**) Millions of computers across the world which are connected together so they can share information.

Internet service provider (**ISP**), **Internet access provider** (**IAP**) A company, with computers that are permanently connected to the *Internet*, which enables you to connect your computer to the *Internet*.

network Computers and computer equipment, such as printers or scanners, that are connected together so they can share information.

newsgroup A group of people who share *e-mail* messages about a particular subject.

offline Not connected to the *Internet*

online Connected to the *Internet*

program A set of instructions that enables you to use a computer to carry out a particular type of task.

search engine (**search service, search index, search directory**) A *program* you can use to look for specific information on the *Web*.

software *Programs* on a computer.

surf To look at *Web pages* on the *Web*.

upload To copy a *file* or *program* from your computer onto another computer which is permanently connected to the *Internet*.

URL (**Uniform Resource Locator**) An *address* of a *Web page*.

virus A *program* which is deliberately designed to damage other *programs* or *files* stored on computers.

Web page A page of information, usually including text and pictures, on the *Web* looked at using a Web *browser*.

Web site A collection of *Web pages* made by the same person or organization, which are linked together by *hyperlinks*.

World Wide Web (**Web, WWW**) Part of the *Internet* which is made up of *Web pages* linked together by *hyperlinks*.

Index

Where there is more than one page listed for a subject, the **bold** numbers show where to find the main pages for that subject.

Acknowledgements
Every effort has been made to trace the copyright holders of the material in this book. If any rights have been omitted, the publishers offer their sincere apologies and will rectify this in any subsequent editions following notification.
Usborne Publishing Ltd. has taken every care to ensure that instructions contained in this book are accurate and suitable for their intended purpose. However, the publishers are not responsible for the content of, and do not sponsor, any Web site not owned by them, including those listed below, nor are they responsible for any exposure to offensive or inaccurate material which may appear on the Web.

Microsoft and Microsoft Windows are registered trademarks of Microsoft Corporation in the US and other countries. All Microsoft screenshots reprinted with permission from Microsoft Corporation.

Cover Globe - European Space Agency/Science Photo Library; Optical disk - Telegraph Colour Library; Hewlett Packard Pavilion Multimedia PC (*also* Title page, p.52) - courtesy of Hewlett Packard; Cyber Tiger **http://www.nationalgeographic.com/tigers/maina.html** - Copyright © National Geographic Society. All rights reserved; astronaut **http://www.askanastronaut.com/** - reproduced with permission of the National Space Society. **Title page** dolphin, astronaut, water, globe - © Digital Vision; bullet train - Telegraph Colour Library/Ken Ross. **p.2** Cannes (*also* p.51) - image courtesy of **www.filmfestivals.com**. **p.3** Planet (*also* p.63) fish (*also* background p.42-43) - © Digital Vision. **p.6** scrolling mouse - Logitech; trackball, touchpad - photos courtesy of Watford Electronics. **p.48** speakers - Gateway; microphone - Logic 3; headphones - AIWA - photograph by Howard Allman. **p51** **http://www.vam.ac.uk** © Victoria and Albert Museum, London, 1999; **http://earth.jsc.nasa.gov** - courtesy of NASA; **http://www.virginradio.com** - image courtesy of Virgin Radio; **http://www.streetmap.co.uk** courtesy of BTEX; **http://www.boardcast.net** - The BoardCAST Network; Toca2 **http://www.gamespot.co.uk/pix** © CODEMASTERS LIMITED; Earthworm Jim **http://www.gamespot.co.uk/pix** © 1998 Interplay Production Game development & software Engine © Vis Interactive. Earthworm Jim is a trademark of Shiny Entertainment. **p.52** globe - © Digital Vision; modem - Hayes; AOL logo - AOL UK; Prodigy Internet logo - used with permission of Prodigy Communications Corporation. Prodigy is a registered trademark, and Prodigy Internet and the Prodigy Internet logo are trademarks, and all are copyrights of Prodigy Communications Corporation in the United States and other countries. **p.56-57** background images - © Digital Vision. **p.60** **http://www.nationalgeographic.com** - copyright © National Geographic Society. **p.61** **http://www.crittercam/index.html**, **http://www.nationalgeographic.com/seas/resources.html**, **http://www.nationalgeographic.com/refuges/index.html**, **http://www.nationalgeographic.com/refuges/c060.html** - copyright © National Geographic Society; **http://www.cmc-ocean.org**, **http://www.cmc-ocean.org/agenda/index.html** - copyright © Center for Marine Conservation. **p.62** Hubble telescope images - Association of Universities for Research in Astronomy, Inc (AURA)/Space Telescope Science Instutute (STScI); background space - courtesy of NASA. **p.65** **http://www.newscientist.com** - Planet Science, New Scientist; **http://www.vogue.com** - CONDÉ NAST PUBLICATIONS LTD; **http://www.virgin.net** - VIRGIN NET, **http://www.bbc.co.uk** - BBC ONLINE, **http://www.raicast.rai.it/intro.htm** - RAICAST. **p.67** Broadcast - Broadcast Net; Sky - SKY ONLINE; LineOne - LineOne Net/SpringBoard Internet Services; NewScientist, BBC, Virgin Net, Vogue - see p.65. **p.70** guitar - © Digital Vision

The publishers would also like to thank Franco Giambalvo for his help with Italian screenshots.